THE CHRONICLES OF
ARIEN

MATHEW LEASK

First published 2017 by Mathew Leask

Copyright © Mathew Leask

The right of Mathew Leask to be identified as the author of this work has been asserted by them in accordance with the Copyright, Designs and Patents Act 1988.

This is a work of fiction. Names, characters, places, and incidents either are the product of the author's imagination or are used fictitiously. Any resemblance to actual persons, living or dead, events, or locales is entirely coincidental.

All rights reserved. No part of this publication may be reproduced, stored in or introduced into a retrieval system, or transmitted, in any form, or by any other means (electronic, mechanical, photocopying, recording or otherwise) without the prior written permission of the author. Any person who does any unauthorised act in relation to this publication may be liable to criminal prosecution and civil claims for damages.

ISBN: 9781973522690

Chapter I
Taste Of Adventure

The dark clouds shrouded the forest in a gloomy fog, like a poisonous gas it seeped down from the sky, with long fingers clawing its way down unsuspecting throats. The trees loomed overhead, casting fearsome shadows across the leaf ridden floor. The forest was still, silent and eerie. Nosver forest had always been this way; most of the visitors to New town avoided the mists fearful of what they couldn't see, of the horrors that lurked within. The forest did not come without large beasts and many fairy tale monsters. Most indeed were harmless tales, like that of the bullfrog who ate children if they didn't eat their greens, yet there were a few tales so gruesomely true that most kept far from the woods. In fact, those affected by the tales pretended the forests themselves were nothing but legends, too afraid to even think of such horrors. Yet there where a select few who cherished the woods, they loved the privacy the mighty trees provided and the serenity that could be found amongst them, not to mention some of the most prized herbs in all of New town. From the cutthroat root, used in the finest ales around lake rose to sharks bark found mainly in the black markets of Mardian. Those who were agile, light and had a skilful eye, of course, could only obtain these herbs. Especially if you wanted to make it out alive.

Orik sat on a stool against the bar of The Broken Axe pub. Everyday Orik sat in this seat; he would drink his ale and would head home. Orik was a Dwarf; he had wiry brown hair that blended with his beard which hung just shy of his belt. He was old but like most dwarves he still had a stocky appearance, he was rather tall by dwarf standards being four foot six. He wore simple clothing; his shirt was green, collared with the pelt of a wolf. His trousers were all different shades of green and brown, although he no longer could tell which brown was cloth and which was dirt, his large iron boots lined with fur too were covered with mud, worn and tattered. He was by no means anything special; he looked like the average dwarf, battle scars and all. Age had tarnished his face with wrinkles around his eyes that blended and merged with the large scar that ran from his forehead to the corner of his mouth, this was a repetitive life but it was time for change.

**

"Are you going to finish that?"
"No I'm just going to go through the effort of getting out of bed, leaving the house, walking two miles to get to my favorite pub to spend my hard earned money to buy a pint of cutthroat beer, and then give it to the likes of you"
"Is that a no then Orik my old friend?"
Orik sighed in frustration.
"Bolger"
Bolger seeing this as an invitation pulled up a chair. Orik did not move, hunched over his pint, he waited for the onslaught of pointless information about to be thrust upon him.
"I have just got back from Nosver, that cutthroat you are drinking was caught by yours truly....."
"It does taste a little off" Orik chuckled at his own remark, but Bolger continued as if he had not heard the insult.
"There I was cutthroat in sight when two, ten foot warbles appeared, bloody screamers, I thought about going home and forgetting the whole thing but, no I wouldn't have been able to live with myself if I had run away, so I took out my axe and ran dead for them" Orik smirked as Bolger rambled on about the

warbles. Remembering the days he too would tell the tales of the perilous Nosver but, he was the most knowledgeable of all when it came to cruel and vicious monsters and all the creatures that dwelled within the darkness.

"So I swung around and buried my axe in its torso the rest of those shades soon disappeared into the night HA! They must have been afraid"

"So two warbles one skane and four shades how ever did you survive"

"Well..." Orik stood up and signaled the elvish barman to put the last two pints on his tab.

"You always were one to run away," Bolger remarked as Orik headed to the door.

Orik whipped around and jumped at Bolger, he evaded the attack and hit into a bar stool consequently sending it spiraling into a young bar maiden. Who like most Dwarven women were not afraid of a good fight. She grabbed Bolger by the ear and began dragging him out the room. Orik laugh along with some of the other patrons and left, as he did so Bolger stumbled to his feet shouting "You wait you old fool you, you BOWLGIAN"

The insult was meant to cut deep into Orik's heart to be called a sympathizer with the race of man was the greatest dishonor to be placed upon a dwarf. Orik did not care he had heard the same insult many times before. When the race of man first set foot upon this land they raged war against the people of Areien. They demolished the holds in Mardian, ripping through the land taking Dwarves, Elves, and Normads with them. Dwarves from all regions joined arms to fight against the evil. Orik, however, did not fight, he was young, and he had made friends with many men. The Dwarves pushed the men back to the highlands but life was never really the same. Orik just accepted the change, for this his family, his friends, and most of Dwarf-kind shunned him. Bowlgian they called him, a sympathizer of man. At first, this confused and upset him but after a while, he came to realize he would never be accepted but he did not dwell as long as he had a good stove a working oven and the best forge in the whole village he was happy. In those days he would make weapons and armour for the warriors, those that would accept in any case. You seldom see Orik's armour around anymore. In the night Orik would enjoy cooking and eating the most adventurous meals concocted from ingredients most Dwarves would not think to use. Cooking was Orik's real passion, but on this night his cooking would have to wait.

When Orik left the pub it took all his strength to stay calm, Bolger's remark had got to him the only thing he had got better at over the years is hiding that fact that it hurt. He walked at a stern pace, nearly tripping on the cobbles beneath his feet. He walked past the well and through the gap in the houses, hopping over the fence that surrounded the village of Rundon. He walked over the great hill dodging the rabbit holes on the ground, he stopped upon the hill. It was quiet. No sounds of metal being beaten, nor drunken brigands falling out of the inn, Orik calmed down and sauntered past the windmill that sat at the peak of the hill where old man Rangnor used to work, in recent times the windmill has fallen into ruin, only disease-ridden animals called it home now. Trees loomed over the cracked path that leads up to the mill door, they were lifeless like skeletons stretching to reach the sky. Orik shivered in fear and scuttled past as quickly as he could, even the bravest souls shudder at the mention of it; he saw the river that would take him out of the borders of this village and then home to Aramoth

When Orik finally got home, after trekking across the river that separated his village from Rundon, he noticed something was different, he had left his home in darkness however, he was sure he could see a light coming from his dining room. He did not move. The thought of someone being in his house shot fear into his heart. He briskly walked to his rusty iron door and twisted the tarnished brass door handle; he slowly opened the door and crept inside. He crept past the front room. It was a large house made of stone and metal. The dark wooden floorboards creaked under his weight. The living room was still, quiet. The table still covered with papers and books, Orik enjoyed reading, but most scriptures were written in elvish making it difficult to find a decent read. The fire was dying out in the chimney, the flickering light cast ugly shadows around the room. The paintings hung on the walls, seemed to be watching him. The curtains look like shades lurking in corners ready to attack. He quickly scanned the room, hoping to dash away, when he noticed the deep red carpet strewn along the floor had moved and the candles hanging over it where lit. Anger began to seep through Orik's veins. He marched down the hallway accepting the living room was empty and headed towards the dining room where he could see the light was coming from. As he turned to go inside his satchel brushed against a table with a vase of flowers on them, but he did not notice, they wobbled and swayed until finally, they came crashing down to the floor with an almighty smash. Orik span round but as he turned he could see someone standing over the wreckage.

"Esian?" whispered Orik with a very bewildered and excited look "Is it really you?"
"Yes, Orik it is me, I am sorry for the intrusion" Esian was a man, one of the tallest of them. He had long black hair and a small but elegantly shaped beard stretching from the bottom of his ears to peak of his chin. The attire in which he dressed was poor, not that of kings or noble folk, it was that of a hunter who bare harsh weathers in the same clothes, covered in mud and leaves. His brown leather jacket was old and worn; it had buckled straps going all the way down the coat. His bow held

in his right hand and a quiver of arrows on his back. On each hip sat large swords, the handles etched with markings Orik did not understand, they must have been crafted in the land of men; Esian's home. Orik stopped and stared for a moment trying to think of a reason why Esian would risk his life just to talk to him.

"I need your help Orik, I was found hunting in the Dwarven lands, I know the laws but the skane I was chasing came across the borders and he had something important of mine. My mother's necklace, he stole it while I was asleep in the wild.

"My friend" sighed Orik "I'm afraid I cannot help you I am too old to go chasing Skanes"

"I know and although that would be a great honor of mine to hunt with you it is not why I am here. I caught the Skane but he bested me and wounded my arm and leg but I cannot let him go" it was only in this moment Orik noticed the blood dripping from his wounds and the drained look upon his face.

"So it is care and armour that you require," said Orik "we shall soon see to that"

"I don't want to put you out Orik" Orik left to room and went to the kitchen. He came back with a bowl of warm water and bandages.

"Why do you have wine?" questioned Esian

"It will clean your wounds" Orik poured the wine on the bandages and the placed them on Esian's skin. The pain shot through him like a sharpened arrow meant for only one person, an arrow that had waited and waited to get sharper and sharper until it finds its victim. Esian did not whimper, did not cry, just simply closed his eyes and tightened his grip on the arm of the chair in which he sat.

"Awfully quiet" Orik enquired

"The more pain I injure now without making a fuss will only make me more efficient in battle" Orik dressed his wounds. By this point, darkness was flourishing and the hour was late they agreed to start on the armour in the morning. They both sat in chairs in the living room drinking a late night tea before bed.

"Do you miss it?" asked Esian
"Miss, what mi'lad?"
"Me, you and Frengar, may he rest in peace, hunting together going on adventures, looking for trouble wherever we could find it"
"No I most certainly do not; coming home battered and bruised always looking over my shoulder"
"You have to admit we had some pretty good times"
"Yes ok, I will admit the times we shared were rather enjoyable. At times"
"How is Rein? I was surprised to not see her here" Orik lost focus of his guest and thought of his wife and how he missed her so. She was beautiful by Dwarf reckoning anyway, she was the most skillful of blacksmiths in her younger days she would help her father in the workshop holding the metal in the fire then cooling it after it had been beaten. She enjoyed it very much but knew there was no place for women in that male-dominated profession. Orik's face rapidly changed he looked at Esian with empty eyes and a vacant expression. "Oh, my friend I am so sorry is it bold of me to ask when and how?"
"Last winter she was too old and she could not fight the ailment that took her"
"She is in a better place now brother she is guiding you in everything you do" The two talked until their mugs where empty, reminiscing about old times they nearly forgot to go to bed.

In the morning Orik awoke to an aroma that would wake any Dwarf, alive or dead, from their slumber. He walked into the dining room and there was an array of salted pork, beef, and bacon and any meat you care to think of.

"To say thank you for taking me in and seeing to my wounds"
"All of this ....for breakfast?"
"Actually it's more like lunch it is not far off midday"
"MIDDAY!" shouted Orik "midday, why didn't you wake me, I need to get started on your armour, how do you want it?" Esian laughed
"Leave the armour, for now, my friend. Eat, you didn't last night so you must be famished my friend" Orik saw his reasoning and sat down. He filled every ounce of his body with the delicious spread Esian had laid out for them.

"Thank you Esian that was quite delicious, now how do you want your armour?"
"Ok I need it to be light, but to protect me, I just need torso and legs no arms"
"Ok stay inside, if you were to be seen..."
"I know, I know" Esian interrupted. Orik walked outside. His forge had once been the largest in the whole of Araket, but times had hit the Dwarven lands and trade to these parts was slim. He decided to use the last of the strange elvish metal which he had stored for a special occasion and this certainly seemed to be such an occasion. Elvish metal was light as a warble would be when stalking its prey but as hard as skane scales. Orik heated it to the temperature he thought appropriate. Beating the metal into the shape of his friend's torso he thought of the battles that it would see and started to doubt his craftsmanship but he did not falter he carried on beating the metal. He then did the back carefully sculpting the shape of Esian's shoulders into the shiny golden surface. Orik thought about putting on the family crest upon the
Armour, but stopped himself, if Esian was ever caught with the Dwarven armour he would be punished by his people as a traitor. Orik fashioned the armour for Esian's legs out of the same metal but did not feel the need to measure him, he knew

in his own mind the size they should be. Orik went inside carrying the wide-shouldered angry looking armour. He found Esian in the kitchen making some tea.
"Well are you finished?" he said softly "You have been gone for many hours"
Orik offered the armour to Esian "well go on then, try it on lad" Esian walked into the upstairs bedroom and he squeezed into the armour contorting any way he could to get it on.
"How is it?" Orik persisted. Esian came through the door with a strange and uncomfortable look on his face. "I said it was meant to be light, it doesn't even fit me properly" Orik face change from excited to angry like the thunder god himself was in the room. Esian spoke quickly.
"But it will do, thank you. I knew I could count on you Orik you really are a very good friend indeed"

Darkness crept back into the village; there was a foul breeze from the north.
"Maybe you should rest here tonight Esian there is a chill in the night it would not bode well for your quest if you left"
"Thank you, my friend, I would very much like to sleep in a comfy bed I suspect it is the last for a long time" Esian finished his tea and went straight to bed leaving Orik down by the fire, he wondered if he could possibly go with Esian on another adventure? Part of him yearned to get away, Dwarves were adventurous by nature, and a life spent in the comfort of home was no life at all. But Orik was old, his back creaked as he walked and his hands were frail. How on earth could he yield an axe now? Orik was barely a Dwarf, he was a man sympathizer and he lived like one. Greedy and comfortable.

Esian woke to bacon and eggs in front of him.
"Just a bit of food to get you on your way laddy. Cant adventure with no food in your belly"
"Thank you very much" Esian took a bite of the food, his face

lit up, the tastes in his mouth danced over his taste buds as if they knew exactly where to land.
"Orik my fellow this is the best breakfast I have ever tasted"
"Thank you, I take pride in what I cook and I do my best, always"
"Well, my friend you have certainly outdone yourself" Esian finished the breakfast with haste. Then began to dread the ordeal of putting on Orik's armour.

It seemed no matter which way he twisted his body the armour would fight against him, he was scared he would do himself an injury before his quest had even begun. Nevertheless, he persisted and finally prevailed. The armour felt as if it would protect him however it was light but it was wearable once on. Esian walked out of the bedroom and into the hall, Orik was waiting for him, he was very good at reading people and he could see that Esian was not at all pleased.
"I know it is not the best armour, but then again I'm not the best blacksmith, I only became a blacksmith to make my family happy. It's even harder to make money now as I'm not popular with the village no one buys my wares. They won't even let me cook in the warrior's hall, apparently, it is dishonorable for me to leave my profession and they would take my house. What am I going to do?"
"my friend you are the kindest dwarf I have ever met not to mention the most intelligent, you will find your way" Orik paused for a moment thinking about Esian's words and what they meant but as he did so Esian started to leave, he picked up his arms lashing his swords to his waist and made for the door.
"What if you're seen?" Esian turned to Orik and smirked
"Orik my friend I will be fine, thank you for your kindness" Esian sneaked out of the door and round the back of the house next to Orik's. Esian began to climb the small hill directly behind the house, it overlooks the village of Aramoth,

Orik's home, it stretched high above the village, their house needn't stretch as high as the hill after all dwarfs where small but sturdy beings and the houses of Aramoth reflected their culture perfectly they were no miners nor great warriors, but farmers of the western region, of course, if their kin from the east requested aid they would once again take up arms but otherwise they were happy being left alone. Esian reached the top of the hill. Just before he disappeared into the distance he turned at looked at Aramoth Orik's house, in particular, a smile grew on his face as he disappeared. Orik was happy to have his house back to normal but he was also saddened by the departure of what seemed to be his only friend.

Days past with no word from Esian. He waited anxiously but still no word, eventually he decided it was best to go back to work and try to make a living not that it was easy with no one buying anything from him anymore, again his thoughts returned to going on an adventure with Esian but again he dismissed it nearly as swiftly as he thought it. He pulled a chair outside and sat next to his front door smoking a pipe, which he often did, watching people go about their daily business. No one would take notice of him anymore as if he was sitting there at all. He watched and saw all manner of people go by, from settled families to folk that were just passing through, some rather stout with weapons an armour but they did not look like the soldiers of the king and some that looked they had gone for a nice walk and simply got lost. It didn't make much of a difference to Orik he was happy just sitting outside his door smoking on his pipe he had no need for company anymore he had grown quite used to having his own space and his own things. It started to get dark, the noise of the busy village soon died and a cold breeze drifted into the village. Orik decided to go inside and go to bed.

Orik shot up. Hearing something rap against the door. TAP. TAP. TAP. He clambered to his feet feeling woozy and unsure. Who would be knocking this late? TAP. TAP. TAP Orik felt an alarming sense of fear creep over his body. He ran out of his bedroom, skidding into the hallway. It felt different somehow as if someone had been here. TAP. TAP. TAP Orik headed for the door, ripping it open. Standing in the moonlight was the silhouette of a man, Orik struggled to his face, he appeared withered and old. Orik reached out his hand to motion the man closer that's when he saw it, the blood-ridden, mangled face he knew so well as the body collapsed into his house he realized. It was Esian.

Orik's eyes quickly open, sweat covered his face. He walked into the dimly lit hallway.
"It was a bloody nightmare" his voice was unsure. He clasped the handle of his front door, yanking it open. Nothing. There was no one nor had anyone been there during the night. He stood for a moment staring out into the cold night, silently wishing that Esian had been there. Feeling a fool he lifted his shoulders before heading into the kitchen to make breakfast. The dream plagued his mind. He could not understand what worried him more, his friend fighting on his own? Or the fact that Orik chose to stay behind? What happened to the young boy, who so valiantly gave up his life for adventure? Who without a second thought would aid his friend in battle? Orik grew tired of the questions that spiraled his mind. One, in particular, ached to be answered more than any other. "Who am I? I am no dwarf if I cannot create armour, no man if I cannot have to courage to aid my friends. No one if I choose a life of solitude" it was this very thought that struck his heart. Orik turned into the large sitting room. Above the large fireplace was a picture, old and dust covered. The man was large, powerful and in his eyes, you could see a life of pain, bravery, and determination. Orik's father bore down on him. "I

will not shame you, I will prove to you that I am worthy of the name Orik Ironfist" the choice was made. Orik darted for his bedroom.

He rushed into his room to grab his old adventuring bag; he found it under his bed. Orik blew the dust off; the bag was old made of green and brown leathers. It was cracked in was falling apart there were small rips that had been notably repaired with needle and thread.
He found some clothes, folded them neatly then put them in. on his way into the kitchen he kicked a chest in the hallway, he had nearly forgotten what was inside. Slowly he lifted the dank old wooden lid, inside was a double-bladed axe that stood nearly as tall as he did, the dust tumbled of it like water on a cliff, attached to the axe was a sheath clearly made for the back of the wearer. Below this axe was a suit of armour gleaming in the candlelight of the house. Orik lifted the armour remembering all the trials it had seen, he cautiously put it on; it did not fit as it used to. He noticed the family crest, in polished bronze it sat upon the breast of the chest plate. It was an anvil outlined in gold with a hammer striking the centre; two axes set in a V shape below the anvil to signify the coming together of his mother's family, who were great warriors, and his fathers, who were great miners. Orik's father, Orgir, was a very good and very well-known blacksmith. He could create the lightest armour and the most beautiful of jewelry in all of Areien. People respected him so much they would just give him recourses and ask for no payment even if they had mined all day to get it, however, this was not true for the rarer of materials. Orik remembered the day Orgir went into Nosver forest behind new town looking for some wood to make a smaller workbench for Orik when a skane attacked and fatally wounded him; he made it back to the house with three limbs intact but his injuries where to great he died only a few days later.

Just before Orik moved into the kitchen to take some food, a shimmer of light caught his eye, he looked back into the chest, he had forgotten about his father's sword. This sword was mighty; the centre of the blade was golden with dwarven runes running up to the top. He pulled it out of the chest with a tight grip strapping it to his waist; he would fight with his father's fury. Orik went into the kitchen to fill what room there was 8in his bag with food, bread vegetables, and mead. He ran out into his long hallway and stood for a moment, uncertain of what lay ahead. He hesitated. He was scared. He used this fear to drive him on. Walking out of his front door he remembered all the times he had spent there all the ups and downs he turning locking his door he looked up at the house, he smiled as if to say goodbye to a very old, very dear friend that he wasn't going to see for a very long time.

Chapter II
Fygir

Orik wondered how he would find Esian and tried to follow the way he went but could not climb what looked like to him an enormous hill it looked like it touched the sky. He would have to walk all the way through the village to the side of the hill where it was lower; he did so noticing that although he was in a shining outfit of armour and had enough weapons to take on a small army, still no one took notice of him. He got to the lowest point of the hill and proceeded to the top. He was hoping to find some sort of sign that said which way Esian went, that maybe there would be some tracks although Esian's tracks looked the same as anyone else's. Unfortunately, though there was nothing, he looked at his village and how small it looked from where he stood. He turned and started to walk. The grass was a beautiful green; it was long and swayed in the wind. As Orik was walking he thought maybe Esian went to new town, maybe someone there had seen him? At night it could be a perilous journey, one he most defiantly did not want to take.

"You can do this, just don't think about it," he said to himself. Reassuring his mind that he would find his friend. After walking for what seemed like hours he finally found a road, more of a path really where people and horses had been and the grass was unable to grow. There was neither stone nor brick on the ground, just dirt. He did not know if this road would take him to new town as he had not done this journey since he was a young boy. After his father died Orik's mother, Liena decided to move to the region of Araket since the memories were too hard to bear. They moved into the blacksmiths quarters in a small village called Aramoth in the south of Araket. They moved here because it was unoccupied and tried to live in peace. She died of old age ten years later. The house fell to Orik. Then men came with their thirsty war. Aramoth was nearly untouched but, as all the other Dwarves went to fight Orik stayed behind. When man set foot in Araket he greeted them with food and hospitality it was because if this they did not send the village into ruin. It was here the friendship between Orik and Esian was forged. Man soon left Aramoth but Esian stayed behind…

The region of Araket was large and it would take Orik a long time to cross into new town. Aramoth and Rundon where the only villages in Araket, there were no towns or cities. It was flat and very green with beautiful rivers and streams sitting parallel to the sea of souls that separated Areien from Noragor, the land of men. Orik found a large broken log laid by the side of the path. Sitting on the log, Orik pulled out a chunk of bread from his bag had whipped out his pipe from his sleeve and had a spot of lunch. Ponies rode by, carrying people on their own business. He thought to ask them where the path leads but never plucked up the courage. Orik enjoyed walking he liked being on the move in the fresh air and the wildlife he would occasionally see. It was the middle of summer and all the trees and flowers were in full bloom the colors and smells were enticing and Orik wished desperately to sleep on them but he wanted to use all the daylight he could and carried on walking until the night crept up on him. He started to look for somewhere to make camp he thought he would go into the wilderness instead of sleeping next to the path, as folk might try to steal his money and food while sleeping. He turned off the path into the dark forest, the trees blocked out the sun. The length of the grass was the perfect height for Orik to lie down and not be seen and that is what he did.

The clouds in the sky darkened and released their rain; it fell like cold stones upon Orik's face and woke him from his slumber. Frustrated by this he angrily got to his feet and marched towards the path, he could see there were more people on the path than in the day before they all had saddened faces and empty eyes, after walking for a little while longer he came to a village much smaller than his own, not worth putting on any map. The houses in this village were falling down, burnt and broken. He walked further, the ground was scorched and bloodstained, he came to what seemed to be the centre. There was a well surrounded by ruins of houses and shops some still lightly smoldering, creating a dense cloud of smoke. He felt a tug on his feet, lying in the dirt was the broken body of a young dwarf, he had bites all over his body and a burnt face. The dwarf child cries shot through Orik's body, he knelt by the child taking him in his arms, clutching him close to his chest.

"Help …please" the child cried Orik recognized the bites, it was the same bites his father had after coming back from Nosver. As a tear rolled down his face he remembered the last words his father had said, the way his eyes had faded of all light the moment the last words escaped his lips. Orik felt the pain of heart-wrenching loss as the words resonated in his head "be brave in the face of evil, but wise in the face death" he had never truly understood the meaning but somehow he knew that his father had chosen those words for a reason. Orik was snapped out of his trance by a piercing scream.

"Help…. Please" Orik ripped a part of his undershirt and soaked it in the well; he soaked child's wounds and shouted for help. Nobody answered. He thought this impossible

"How can there be no one here?" he said under his breath to himself. The child started to lose consciousness, Orik panicked.

"Stay with me" he shouted "don't give up" the child's eyes slowly opened. Orik took him in his arms and ran for the safest house, he kicked the door open, surprised to see people inside, a dwarf male and female hiding in the corner as if afraid to be seen by anything or anyone

"I need help, this child is dying," Orik said as he fell to his knees. The two dwarfs jumped to their feet, the woman disappeared into another room and the other took the child off Orik. He laid him on a table in what looked like a dining room but had no paintings; no chairs, not even a sideboard to hold plates or other things one might find in a dining room.

"It's going to be alright Fygir I promise," said the dwarf to the child. Fygir was fair-haired, blonde. Through the blood pouring down his face blue eyes shone, he could have been no older than 12, but his eyes told a story of pain that only old war men should tell.

"You know him?" exclaimed Orik in frustration. Why didn't they act as soon as they saw him?

"Yes he is our neighbor's child, I am Darek and my wife is Lien" Lien walked into the room with numerous towels and a bowl of warm water, she wrapped the towels around the broken and injured Fygir. He winced at every touch as if his own body was made out of pain. He cried several times. The cries pierced the hearts of those around him. Darek and Orik walked through the archway into the kitchen. Orik noticed there was nothing in there either, no pots or pans, no spices or food.

"What happened here?" Orik whispered.

"Skanes" replied Darek "in the night, they came with no sound. They took people and stole all they could carry but before they left, they didn't think they had caused enough destruction, they butchered people and burnt their homes there where only a couple of survivors, as soon as we heard the commotion we hid in the cupboard, we heard them come in and take all of our belongings we were lucky they heard the call from their leader before they opened it or we would not be speaking now and our fate would be the same as the boys"

"Skanes? This far from Nosver... how?" Orik's anger stirred

inside him. He hated the Skanes, nasty, scaly beings as tall as a man but they only knew how to hate and kill, they were vicious feared by all in Areien. If anyone was lucky or skillful enough to kill a Skane they could sell their skin on the black market and eat for a year. Normal traders would not buy them as they were thought to bring bad luck to anyone who touches them but if you find yourself face to face with a Skane then your luck cannot get much worse. Darek did not know how they had got this far without being detected and killed, but they did and this did not bode well for Orik's journey.

Fygir's cries subsided, Darek and Orik hearing this darted for the dining room; tears fell from Lien's eyes. The boys eyes turned to glass, as he drew his last breath he looked at Orik, the boy shed no tears and had no fear in his eyes but Orik saw the last look of a boy who had nothing to lose he was not afraid of death he welcomed it for the pain he was feeling could be no worse than death, Orik knew then what he must do he must not be fearful. He must be brave. As life deserted the child's body his eyes slowly closed, his hands fell open and a broach struck the floor. Orik knelt down. Taking the object in his hand. Turning it over in the sliver of light that cut across the room. It was a silver circle with spiked edges and an anvil in the middle no hammer striking it or metal bent over it just an anvil. Orik's did not recognize this family crest.
"That's strange though the crack in the cupboard door I caught a look at some of the Skanes, that crest was burned into their backs, the exact same symbol," said Darek
"We need to bury him," said Lien with a choke in her throat and tears racing down her face.
"Yes Lien you are right," said Orik "do you have a shovel we can use?" after that no small talk was shared nor eye contact made. They walked with their heads bowed. Orik offered to carry Fygir. They took him to a hill that sat close to the village. They buried him just before dusk and fashioned a marker out

of wood that was left from his home. It was in the shape of an eagle to signify the courage of the child in the face of death. Orik stayed with Darek and Lien that night but no dinner was made, no song was sung and the only conversation was that of a bid goodnight.

Orik woke to an empty house nobody was around, no Darek and no Lien he did not understand why. He walked into each room searching for some sort of sign or a note.
"Why would they just leave without even a goodbye?" he said to himself. He walked out of the house into the dirty burnt village. It was deserted. Vacant of life. He walked through the village and noticed a signpost. An arrow pointing back to his village and another point down the road reading New Town.
"A bit of luck at last" Orik followed the path, as he walked he turned and looked at the hill where Fygir was buried, no expression was on his face, he just, looked, and remembered.

The road was long and tedious it was full of inclines and descents some very steep and slippery from the rain that had still not dried where the sun could not reach. He reached the highest point on the road he could see above the tree tops and could see the snow-capped summits of the majestic eagle's peak. The mountains that sat at the top of Arien where beautiful, huge in size and in reputation. They were treacherous, some would try to climb them but the face where never seen again nor their voices heard they simply disappeared from existence. Darkness sneaked up on Orik once more, he had actually been walking in the darkness for three hours but was so deep in thought he did not notice, the only thing the alerted him to the time was the fatigue he felt. He walked into the wilderness and laid on the ground. He missed the comfort of his nice warm bed and it would not be the last time he would feel this way.

The sound of howling pierced Orik's ears. Darkness still shrouded the world. His eyes opened and he jumped to his feet. The pound of his heart drowned out the sound of his panicked breathing. He took his sword from its scabbard and waited...nothing. No sound just silence. This frightened him more, sweat fell from his brow like rainwater dripping of tree leaves. Standing there waiting for the uncertain, Orik thought of his friend, if he had gone with Esian maybe he would not be facing the ordeal. Without warning, Fygir entered his mind. Courage started to consume Orik's heart. He stopped shaking, his breathing slowed. Another howl reached him, he could tell it belonged to wolf it was closer this time. He could hear them walking, growling at the dinner they were about to receive, a wolf confronted Orik. Eyes like an abyss, black and full of fury. Its fur was coarse and brown with muscle bulging through. Laden with scares. the white-toothed demon jumped at Orik, with a grunt Orik moved but fell to the ground. The wolf seeing his opportunity and pounced at Orik, he rolled and got to his feet. The grey demon snapped his head round and looked Orik in the eyes thrusting fear into his heart without his consent. Orik swung his sword in a panic making no contact with his foe. The wolf retaliated scratching Orik's arm with is metal like claws knocking him off balance, Orik fell on his back with his sword in the air, the wolf jumped after him impaling itself upon it. Blood dripped from its body as it slid down the blood-soaked sword, still snapping its jaws as it died. The colour seemed to disappear from its eyes. Its jaws stopped. They were face to face now, so close Orik could smell its last breath. Orik dropped it to the floor retrieving his sword, the adrenaline so fresh in his veins he started to shake. The pain of his wound soon set in, he took out one of his tunics from his bag and wrapped it around his arm, squeezing it he winced and sat down on his bag a smoked on his pipe. The sun bled over the horizon, dawn was not far away, so he picked himself up and walked towards the great capital of Arien.

The battlements of the wall around New Town soon started to show themselves on the horizon. The wooden gate was large and sturdy with bronze struts going horizontally across the width of each door. They were open but were shut at night, after word reached them of the skane attack close by. Guards, dressed in shining steel armour, patrolled the top and bottom of the wall; they all carried battle horns in case an attack was made. The all had shields in the shape of kites they wear mainly wood but braced with steel around the outside and down the middle, it was bolted to the wood with the strongest of metal bolts, the shimmered in the rising sun. Orik walked into the city the tall buildings stretch over him. Most of them were stone built with wooden supports. He was in awe of the sheer size of the city for a moment he forgot why he came to new town in the first place. He walked through the streets noticing the noise and mostly the rudeness of people just pushing past him as if they were rushing to the bedside of a dying loved one. Dwarfs, Elves and a few men roamed the city streets, huge cobbles lay beneath Orik's feet. Stables lay after the immediate houses behind the gate with horses and ponies tied up with hay below their hoofs and a food trove in front of the house connected.

Chapter III
Searching

Orik found himself in front of a building that was signed as 'The Poison Oak Inn' the sign was protruding from the top of the front door and it was shield-shaped, made of wood with a brown background, a greet oak tree was on either face. The door was tall brown and wooden. Orik opened the door and the sound of a thousand warbles flooded out and positively slapped Orik in the face, the smell of honey roasted ham filled his nose, a smile slowly grew on his face as the sound of laughter welcomed him into the inn. He walked up to the bar to be greeted by a large bald man, a silver beard rested on his round belly. Stains covered his white apron.
"What'll it be me, fellow," he said leaning over the bar looking down on Orik.
"w-w-well have you got any cutthroat" Orik whimper stunned at the men allowed to road freely and at how polite this particular one was being, especially to a dwarf.
"HA!" the barman chuckled "have we got any cutthroat I'm afraid it is all we sell here other than tap water o'course" the barman put a pint on the bar "that's one silver piece, please. Orik handed over one silver piece and two bronze.
"For being so polite, I have noticed that manners are few and far between as of late" The barman smiled and walked to serve an elf who stood next to Orik. He walked to a corner and sat down in the shadows trying not to be noticed; he pulled his pipe from his sleeve and started to smoke, he drank his beer while watching people fall over each other as night drew closer. Some dwarfs started to dance in the middle of the floor their cutthroat fueled jigs where amusing for all in the inn, some lost their balance and crashed to the ground but soon

picked themselves up and began to dance again. Orik walked back up to the bar to ask how much it was for a room for the night.

"Two gold pieced good sir" the barman replied Orik was astonished at the price but had no other choice he paid the fee and went up the bed soon after. Sleep evaded him for most of that night the noise from downstairs kept his eyes from shutting and thought of Esian and Fygir son re-entered his mind. He fell asleep in the early hours of the morning, meaning he woke up horribly late; the left Orik's mood somewhat dismal. He marched downstairs to find the inn empty it was only midday.

"Is lunch to be served soon?" Orik asked

"Yes, certainly what would you like, we have bacon, sausages, and egg or you can have a sandwich with any filling"

"Do you have any salted pork?"

"We do have salted pork I will just get that for you know, names Vigor by the way"

Vigor went out into the back to prepare Orik's lunch. Orik went and sat at the very same table in which he sat the night before. Smoking on his pipe, he felt very uneasy; the inn was eerie when it was empty. Vigor soon appeared with Orik's meal the smell was divine. Orik rummaged around in his coin pouch to pay.

"No charge, it is included in the price of the room," said vigor. Orik smiled and put his coin pouch in his bag, his cheeks started to go red. He felt a little silly. After he finished the meal Orik went to bar to ask vigor if he had seen or heard anything of Esian.

"Now that you mention it I do remember seeing one of my kind in here a couple of weeks ago. He had strange armour I had not seen like of it in my lifetime he was trying to recruit mercenaries for reasons I do not know, I remember hearing something about Nosver.

"Thank you, thank you very much," said Orik getting a bit

ahead of himself "do you know where he went"

"I'm afraid not he didn't tell me anything of his business, I just overheard them while I brought the drinks. But you can try speaking to old man Lienik as I saw the man you speak of go into his shop to buy some weapons" Orik's face looked a little less excited but happy for the information and happy he was on the right track at least.

Orik walked out of the inn bidding the jolly barman goodbye. He headed straight for the shop vigor mentioned. He found the shop; it was tiny no bigger than Orik's own house.

"How can this be a weapons shop," he asked himself. Inside, old man Lienik stood, behind him racks and racks of swords, axes, knives and other more imaginative weaponry. Glass cases of precious weapons lined the sides up to counter and behind, a spiral staircase rose from the floor. Orik greeted Lienik with a smile

"Yes?" Lienik enquired

"I am looking for a man I wonder if you have seen him?"

"I see many folks come and go, day after you will have to be more specific"

"Y-yes of course about two and half weeks ago h-he is tall with thick long black hair wearing strange armour a black beard he has also and maybe a bandage on his right arm"

"AH! So you must be Orik of Aramoth"

"Y-yes that be me"

"And the man you are looking for is Esian"

"YES! YES! Esian you've seen him" Orik came to the conclusion that for some reason Esian had told Lienik of him.

"Well, then these are for you" Lienik handed to Orik a cloak made of the finest wool, colored in green and fell off his shoulders landing just short of the ground. Orik looked back up at the shopkeeper only to have a brand new axe thrust in front of him.

"This was forged just yesterday morning: Lienik grinned as Orik's eyes widened the excitement grew inside him. A new axe to a dwarf was like a newborn baby, it was perfectly balanced with a wooden stave, two leather hand grips sat in perfect distance from each other to get the best grip upon it. With his name in dwarven runes etched into it. Orik's face turned sour.

"I'm afraid I cannot pay you"

"HA! It is ok my friend, Esian paid for everything"

"ALL?" said Orik with raised eyebrows.

"There is more" Lienik chuckled and reached behind him to take a sword from the rack again with Orik's name engraved on the blade. It was light, it shone in the midday sun flooding in through the open door and the hand grip was made of sturdy but soft leather. The old shopkeeper parted Orik from his old weapons.

"NO!" Orik shouted with burning eyes. Ripping his father's sword from Lienik's hand. "I would like to keep this"

"Very well, forgive me I meant no offence" Lienik said as he handed Orik a dagger that slipped into his boot.

"I will keep your axe for when you return"

"If...I return, thank you very much for the weapons and the cloak I shall be on my way now"

"Do you not want to know where Esian has gone, that is why you came is it not?"

"Yes you are right"

"He has gone deep into Nosver. He wanted you to have the weapons, to be ready if you decided to follow him"

"Thank you, Lienik ill buy you a drink sometime"

"I shall hold you to that Orik, my friend"

Orik turned to leave he walked through the door closing it behind him. His face dropped. 'Nosver' he thought, 'it had to be Nosver'. From a small hill in the city, you could see the treetops of the vast and mighty Nosver. The green leaves seemed to shimmer in the sunlight. The evil in that place still pierced Orik's heart and invaded his mind. He feared the forest more than most. Still, he decided to journey to the forest just to make sure Esian was ok. The journey would take less than a day as the forest sat close to the back of new town; so close barricades where situated at the rear gate for fear of the beasts of Nosver wandering too close to the city.

Orik reached the rear gate; it was smaller to the front, much smaller but patrolled by double the guards. A guard approached Orik.
"Where ye be off to laddy?" he said in a hardy northern voice
"I am journeying to Nosver"
"Are you sure, I cannot stop you laddy but dangers beyond imagining lie deep in the darkness of the forest" Orik's voice turned stern
"I KNOW WHAT IM DOING!"
"All right, all right no need to get angry; I'm just doing my job"
"Yes I know I'm sorry, I'm a little nervous"
"Ok then be on your way," Orik said goodbye to the guard. With each step, fear grew bigger and bigger until it nearly turned him around. As he approached the forest it seemed to double in size the trees looked alive in the wind and the inside of the forest seemed to darken, as he made his way through the thick grass that seemed to grab and pull his feet, the sight of New Town soon faded. He pulled out some bread from his bag and ate while he walked, he did not want to stay still for long as something could creep up and attack him. He decided not to rest tonight he would not sleep until he had found company. He did not like the thought of being alone and unaware.

Sword in hand Orik slowly walked forward into the wilderness. Unwelcome sounds came from all around; he did not know what they were, some came closer some moved further away. He began to sweat. The night closed in. the air turned cold.

Orik could see his breath move in the night air. Each step seemed to make a louder noise than the last. The sound of his armour clashing together was louder than he had previously noticed.

Breathing. Loud breathing could be heard from behind him. He froze. Whatever it was it was big. Orik could hear no other sound now just the breathing of some large beast behind him, he found the strength to turn his gaze, looking behind him he saw…nothing, no beast. His body followed, then again the breathing started behind him Orik whipped round, again … nothing. The trees seemed to grow. The darkness, darkened and the crescent moon disappeared from sight. Orik's vision was limited now; he had to rely on his other senses. He could not see the beast nor smell it, but he could still hear it. Its breaths taunted him, with every turn it moved. Then from nowhere, it was above him. Orik not being able to take it anymore turned and ran, his body was not used to running under the weight he carried this slowed him, but by no means was he slow. He ran into broken branches and fallen vines he turned to look back a shadow was in pursuit. Orik's legs kept going and he was slowly entering the infamous fog of Nosver. The fog that never seems to dissipate, the fog that chocked and suffocated its victims. Orik could see nothing. He stopped. Waited. There was no sign of the unknown beast. Nor could he hear it. Orik had thought that maybe he did not want the hassle and had given up and maybe he could stop being scared now, his breathing slowed and his legs stopped shaking. Suddenly from nowhere, an almighty warble scream came from in front of him. Orik fell to one knee not being able to take the piercing scream from the tall dark skinned warble, with eyes like gold, standing over him, the scream got even more defining. He managed to muster the strength to swing his sword. Not having the strength to hold on to it, it slipped from his grasp and flew towards the warble, it sliced its throat leaving it voiceless, its knees cracked as they hit the floor, and it fell to the ground as the last of its scream was exhaled and life vanished from it. Orik stayed on the ground paralyzed by fear. His breathing as fast as the war drums of old. His face transfixed on the dead warble. Still. Silent.

Orik got to his feet staring at the body. He walked to where his sword had landed, picking it up he wished he was back at home with a warm meal and a warm bed not nasty, warble, Skanes or any other unwelcome monsters lurking in the dark. Sheathing his sword he walked once again, still shaking from his ordeal. He walked through the night dodging the moss and vines that seemed to reach out and grab him every minute. His walking pace slowed as his energy ran low. He knew he would have to sleep at some point, but he thought he might find Esian just before he had to, however, Nosver was mighty and Esian could be anywhere. His weapons and Armour doubled in weight and his eyelids soon felt very heavy indeed. He did not know his way, stumbling on protruding roots and rocks he made his way through the suffocating fog. It was so think he could no longer see his hand stretched out in front of him. His skin crawled as the forest stretched around him, he did not know what else to do, crippled from exhaustion he fell on the floor and sleep took over his body. He did not intend for it too but his body was too tired. He did not dream that night for he was too tired and slept too deeply, so deeply in fact that he could not feel himself being picked up and carried through the woods. His arm fell from the blanket in which his kidnapper dragged him, still, he did not wake. The change in temperature as he was laid down by a burning fire still did not wake him...

Orik leaped to his feet and drew his axe. His eyes took time to adjust making him feel helpless. The flames of the fire licked his face; between the hands like wisps of smoke, he could see a man. Head to toe in black he appeared 10 foot tall. "Who are you?!" Orik demanded.

"Relax brother" the voice sent a wave of ease over Orik's body, his eyes focused on the figure before him, noticing only now the armour and weapons. The man was of normal height and well built; covering his face with a hooded cloak, but the voice was clear as day to Orik.

"Esian?"

"You going to the lower that axe or what?" Esian chuckled

Orik slid the axe over his shoulder and smiled at his friend, "I take it you didn't buy that cloak?"

"Well, now that would be telling" the two friends sat by the fire, watching the flames dance in the moonlight. Orik wished he could explain all that he had seen on his journey but a part of him knew that Esian had experienced something similar. The cuts on his arms were fresh and his hands were burned and blistered. Esian had been fighting, fighting creatures so much worse than wolves and warbles.

"I had mercenaries, 5 from Mardian all were taken in the night by Skanes" Esian must have noticed Orik staring at his wounds.

"On the road from Aramoth, a group of Skanes attacked a village, stole the citizens away at night"

"Skanes that far south is troubling, but stealing people away? I don't understand, what happened to the Skanes of Nosver that ripped the bones out of people's skin?" Esian was deep in thought. Orik knew exactly what he was thinking or sensing, there was a force in that forest plotting and planning in the dense trees.

Orik sat next to the campfire, watching, waiting. Whilst Esian slept. The moon was high in the night sky by now but Orik was yet to feel tired. Orik leant over to wake Esian him for his watch; they exchanged a few polite words before Orik huddled up by a tree. Although his mind was wild with thought his body was stolen into a dreamland.

The sun splintered through the trees, making the forest appear almost peaceful, beautiful. The rays of lights danced over Orik's eyes gently rising him from his sleep. Soon his other senses caught up, the sweet smell of appleberry wafted past him. Orik rolled over clicking his spine.
"Appleberry and mustard?" Orik said as he was drawn to the smell.
"Only the finest for you my friend" Esian was stirring the sweet mixture in a wrought iron pot. It was the traditional food of Mardian often served over meat. "caught a few rabbits if you want to skin them over the fire" Orik drew the knife from his boot and grabbed the spine of the dead rabbit with one fell swoop he cut off its head and peeled the skin back cutting it off as he lopped off the animal's tail. He did the same with the other. Esian looked in astonishment as he observed the skill in which Orik did this. He took the rabbits from Orik and put them on a branch that he fashioned as a skewer and placed them over the fire. The aroma filled the air swooping its way into Orik's and Esian's nostrils. Their stomachs ached for the meal they were about to receive. They ate their meal with great speed feeling the flavors dance on their tongues.

Orik stretched up, his bones ached and his joints cracked like thunder.
"Sleeping on the floor is taking its toll on me, I am not as young as I used to be," Orik said while yawning. Esian looked at him and laughed.
"You really are a silly old man but the best I have ever known"
"You are a funny man Esian. Anyway, where are we off to?"
"North, it went north"
"let's go we are wasting time" Orik and Esian walked in the mud talking as if they were in a homely tavern, speaking of the local affairs and such things just as men do when there is nothing to talk about, they began to talk of the weather and how angry it looked on this day. Orik wondered about his

home and if it was still the way he left it. Rain clouds gathered above them, they tumbled over each other like drunken old men. The raindrops fell and flew through the air like an army of arrows, they broke on the canopy of Nosver like ale that has been spilt on a boot. Slowly the leaves got heavy and the canopy opened and large heavy droplets fell on Orik and Esian. They ran and looked for cover, but they couldn't run for long a deep river ran through the center of Nosver and they were now standing on the brink. As the rain fell; the river rose they both knew this but had nowhere to run they didn't want to go back the way they came this would impede their progress too much. They decided to follow the bank for as long as they were able. They ran along the edge looking forward to see if there were any sign of the river getting shallower but there was no such sign. After a while, they grew tired of running as they didn't see the point they were wet now and there was no escaping it. Before they knew it the sun was setting, they knew they had to find somewhere suitable to sleep. They walked for another hour or so until Orik spotted something in a break of the tree line that ran parallel to the river, he did not know what it was, but it put him on edge. As his curiosity took him closer he started to make out the outline of a small cave opening.

"Esian! I have found a place to slee…" Orik turned around to see that Esian was not behind him and that he had wandered off without Esian noticing.

"Esian!" he shouted "where are you! Esian! Answer me" Orik panicked. He ran as fast as he could back to the river bank.

"What is it Orik?"

"Oh, Esian you didn't half give me a fright then laddy. I have found a cave that will do us for the night" they both walked up to the abyss that was the cave. Pure darkness lay in front of them. Almost simultaneously they drew their weapons, Orik his axe and Esian his bow. Esian favored his bow for it allowed him to hit his enemies before they could even see him. Because he used his bow often he was skilled, very skilled he once hit a deer that had disappeared from sight. He was tracking it when he accidentally cracked a branch as he got close and this spooked the deer. Esian stood, followed it with his bow and ass it disappeared into the mist he released his arrow and he walked over to where he fired it, there in the dirt laid a deer with Esian's arrow piercing its eye.

Orik stood in front of the cave wielding his axe while Esian stood behind with an arrow knocked this was would make it easy to hit any enemy that came out of the darkness as Orik only stood just a bit higher than Esian's belt buckle. They edged towards the cave eye wide and senses alert. They soon disappeared from sight darkness shrouded them. Once they were happy that there was nothing in the cave that intended to do them harm Orik went for firewood and they made a fire inside the wet logs took time to light but Esian was a skilled survivor. As the fire grew and the light blossomed they could see that it was a small cave in any respect it stretched high above them and the cave went further and further underground. They took the reserves of food they had from their packs and had supper. Orik wanted to ask what ordeal Esian had faced since he last saw him but daren't, he did not want to upset his friend. Slowly they fell asleep in the security of the cave.

A cold wet hand clasped Orik mouth, as his eyes shot open and his hand grabbed his sword, he could see that it was Esian bent over him making sure he made no sound. He gestured to the mouth of the cave as a group of Skanes walked by. Their scales glistened in the rain and their yellow reflective eyes scoured the area for victims who they could relieve of their life, they were branded with the same mark as the broach Orik carried, they were tall, taller than Esian and their legs bulged with muscles. They walked slowly and

calmly. Their claws were diamonds, sparkling in the moonlight, like small swords extruding from the hands of the beasts. They drifted past the cave taking no notice of it. Orik and Esian breathed a sigh of relief. They did not know if they would be able to fight 12 fully grown Skanes and prevail. Orik took out the broach, which he kept in the inside pocket of his cloak, and showed it to Esian.
"Do you recognize this?"
"It is the same marking that is branded on the back of the Skanes"
"I found it in a village that had been attacked by Skanes similar to the ones we just saw"
"So they are organized," said Esian "I don't understand" Orik could not come up with any sort of explanation and Esian could not either. Orik volunteered to take watch for the rest of the night. Sitting in the darkness his thought returned to his home and how much he missed it. He thought most of the picture of his wife in the dining room and how much he missed her. She would have persuaded him to stay home and not to go on this dangerous endeavor but as he thought this he realized the amount of exhilaration and enjoyment he was getting out of it and how much he liked being with his old friend again. But he would have listened to his wife, he cherished her and everything she did. It was soon sunrise it was in this moment that the forest could look beautiful as the sun bursts through the trees before it rises above the canopy. Orik woke Esian.
"It's time wake up laddy" Esian eyes shot open as he sat bolt upright taking a sharp intake of breath.
"The faces, the faces of the five mercenaries I led to death. I see them" the tear from his eyes mixed with the sweat from his brow.
"It was not your fault Esian there was nothing you could do"
"Revenge, that is what I can do"
"Revenge is not the answer my friend I hate them too. I want

them to pay as much as you but we must be smart about this. If there is an army do you really think we can both take them down together, alone? No, we couldn't so we need help."

"You are right my friend thank you very much, we shall go to new town and seek help, but first my mother's necklace"

"Yes, what we are here for in the first place" Orik packed up his things as did Esian and they left the dank cave behind them the rain still poured which made it impossible to cross the river.

"Maybe there is a bridge somewhere down river," said Orik as he scoured the landscape. In a break in the clouds, the summit of eagles peak could be seen the sun shining on the snow making them look more beautiful than ever. Orik remembered a story that his mother used to tell him about the evil monsters that dwell in the labyrinths that lay inside of eagles peak, beasts that could kill you just by looking at you and make even the most mighty of warriors flee in terror. But Orik dismissed them as just a child's tale. As they walked the ground rose above the height of the river. Esian saw a shadow on the other side. It looked like the silhouette of a dwarf man running on the other side. Esian matched his pace. Orik could not see what Esian was looking at but he ran alongside him anyway, the branches of the trees scratched Esian's face as he sprinted but he did not alter his course.

"There!" Orik shouted as a bridge came into view. The two darted for it running even faster than before to beat the shadow there and see who it belonged to. They ran across the bridge to be greeted by. Nothing. There was no one no dwarf nothing.

"I saw something I promise you it was right here"

"Esian you are tired you're......" Esian's tone changed his voice was stern

"I know what I saw!"

"Don't you take that tone with me laddy, it doesn't matter now Esian we are across the river and we can carry on going north"

"I apologize, friend, I am just…"

"I know laddy. Let's go" Orik accepted Esian's apology. The two walked through the tree line, the midday sun was nonexistent, under banishment from the trees. There was a strange stench in the air it attacked the inside of Orik's and Esian's nostrils. Roots bulged from the ground, tripping them up making it difficult to walk. Suddenly the clashing of swords could be heard close by. Esian was the first to react, darting simultaneously to where the sound was emanating. Orik then followed behind not being so quick to react as he was not sure if it was wise to pounce on danger so obviously. He thought it would have been better to approach silently and see what it was rather than going in blind but he was not going to let his friend run into danger unaccompanied. When they reached the source of the sound there was a man and a Liniech fighting.

Chapter IV
Dangerous Secrets

Orik and Esian froze. Liniechs were feared. They were grown in the darkness of the Barrow Mountain where they dwelled in the damp learning of the stars and the essence of life. They were believed to have settled on the planes of Areien nearly 400 years ago before even Dwarves had claimed the lands. No one really knew why, some believed they were fleeing a darker power but regardless they were skilled fighters, quicker than any other being. All were female with pale skin that was almost luminescent, tall and thin. If it wasn't for their eyes you would be easily fooled into thinking they were human. But their eyes were alien, like pools of mist, white as snow but somehow they dripped darkness. As time passed people grew weary of them and their magic, they spoke of end days and wars and pain, they could read your thoughts and see your fears with one touch, it was believed they could see every moment of your existence. So disjointed from civilization they became like shadows watching in the darkness, waiting. Orik grabbed at his axe, knowing full well against her it would be useless. Esian wandered forward, "you fool don't you know what that is?" Orik whispered harshly as Esian made his way towards the girl.

Orik stared at her unsure if she knew he was there, her hair was jet black and hung loosely in a braid. She was thin and pale, in the light of the moon she appeared cat-like with leather bindings pulled tightly around her torso; shimmering with a dark green tinge. She had a knife hidden with her clothing around her ankle, that matched the large curved blade in her hand. Both where pristine with dark green wrappings for a handle. Orik knew what she was, as a child, he had been fascinated by the tales of her people, he had spent many days hoping to see one. He crept into the tree line where Esian was waiting in the shadows, apparently having lost his confidence to approach her.

"Her eyes" Esian was staring intently at the girl "they don't glow, she can't be a Liniech" only then did Orik notice the mask that covered her eyes, fastened to her left ear. Large raven feathers spread across her eyes all tipped with a hint of green, they covered her eyes completely leaving only her nose and mouth to be seen.

"The mask must cover them Esian, believe me, she is dangerous"

"She is just a girl Orik, she might need our help" before Orik could drag Esian away he had already made his way towards her. Orik lunged after him plowing through the foliage to stop him before it was too late. Esian stepped out from the tree line just as the girl plunged her knife into him. Orik crumbled as he heard the deafening scream that escaped Esian's lips.

"Let him go you vile creature" Orik felt an immense wave of anger flood his veins.

"He won't die, the blade rests nicely 1 centimeter above his heart" her voice was like silk, bewitching and enchanting the man she had previously been fighting made his escape.

"Remove your blade or I'll cut your head off!" the girl laughed lightly to herself infuriating Orik even more. Esian was kneeling on the floor, his head hanging low. She lifted her foot to his shoulder and using his body as leverage pulled the blade from his chest. The cut was perfectly clean.

"You know, I could kill you instantly" she placed the blade in a holder that hung from her hip. She then swung a bag over her shoulder and pulled out a roll of bandage and a small vial of red liquid.

"What are you doing" Orik grabbed his friend and attempted to pull him to his feet

"I'm trying to help him unless of course, you have a better

way" she poured the vial into the wound; Orik nearly ripped it from her hand but was stopped as he noticed the wound began to change. The blood stopped pouring and it began to slowly shrink. She then wrapped the bandage around the wound and put the stuff away. As Esian clambered to his feet the strange woman took off her concealing mask wincing as she did so.
"Ebonyr and you are?" the two recoiled in horror as they saw the white pools that were her eyes. The very eyes the shot fear into the hearts of every soul that lived and breathed. Esian stumbled over his words.
"We-well I'm Esian and this is my companion Orik" Orik shot Esian a stern look. He did not approve of their names being divulged so freely.
"So come on then lass who are you and what you be doing in these parts?"
"Me? I ask you master dwarf what are you doing here?" Orik huffed as he watched himself kick the ground.
"We are on a quest, looking for my mother's necklace but I fear we have stumbled on something much more sinister"
"Do you happen to be tracking a Skane northward?"
"Yes. How could you possibly know that?"
"I am also tracking a Skane that came this way for he stole something of mine also"
"Come on then let's get on with it you can either come with us lass or be on your own" Orik did not like Ebonyr much. He thought there must have been a reason for the man attacking her. Orik did not trust her at all, Esian, on the other hand, could barely take his eyes off her, he was mesmerized by her beauty and the angelical nature in which she moved. As they walked Ebonyr put her mask back on shielding her eyes.
"How is your shoulder Esian?" Ebonyr inquired
"Oh, its fine can't feel it anymore thank you for asking" Ebonyr looked back at Orik, who was walking at a slower pace behind them and smirked. The watchful nights closed in and Ebonyr

took off her raven feather and sighed with a smile.
"That's better" she murmured
"Pardon" Orik jumping at the first chance to find weakness
"It's nothing......."
"Shh" Esian said staring into the darkness this being the only time he has taken his eyes off Ebonyr. Esian kneeled down motioning everyone else to do the same.
"What is it Esi...."
"Shhh!" rustling could be heard in the wilderness. The darkness got darker. The breathing of the Man Dwarf and Liniech seemed as loud as a hundred warble screeches. Esian caught the unmistakable glint of a Skanes eye in-between the trees, his whole body started to shake; he turned to the others and alerted them to it. They all made their body's smaller hoping to go unnoticed by the enemy. This, however, was futile the enemy already knew of their presence. Orik started to crawl silently in the grass in a direction he thought to be away from the beasts. The others cautiously followed. The enemy watched. Waited. In the blink of an eye, there was a pair of dark scaly feet standing before Esian, he looked up to find a Skane mid swing about to decapitate Esian when a small dagger shot into the neck of the beast killing it outright. It couldn't scream as the dagger had all but ripped its vocal cords in half. The blue blood covered Esian hair and face. The stench was near unbearable making Orik cough. They all froze. Reptilian shrieks could be heard in the darkness with every second they got closer and closer Ebonyr was the first to stand up and look around to see what danger was near. All that could be seen was the eyes that seemed to be floating only meters away, half a dozen eyes now surrounded them. Esian flipped the body of the dead skane to find the all-new common brand upon its back. Fear flooded his face and sweat flooded his armour. Adrenaline pumped through his body as he shot up. Orik still lying down did not want to see the horror that awaited him but soon his loyalty to his friend took over.

They all stood back to back waiting for the onslaught that was about to come their way. The eyes got closer soon to be joined by floating pearl white teeth grinning in the darkness. Their breath was foul and could be smelt from where the three where standing. Esian drew an arrow and knocked it in his bow pointing it directly at the middle of a pair of the eyes, Orik took out his axe from his shoulder sheath and Ebonyr drew two fighting knives from her waist. They all prepared for battle. They all whispered to one another.
"Ready"
"Aye"
"Ready"
"Yes"
"Then what are we waiting for"

Esian released his deadly arrow as he did so the pair of eyes disappeared. The others soon bolted for them running at them from every direction. They wielded no weapons for their claws were strong and sharp enough to pierce the broadest of armour and their scales were strong enough that they did not need armour. Before they knew it the Skanes were upon them. As they got closer Ebonyr could see them clear as day one ran directly for her it was fast, as it got close to her she moved to the side leaving her foot behind making thud on the floor and she drove both knives into its torso dropping to one knee to make the impact able to penetrate its thick scales. Another was soon behind her but Orik made short work of it by plunging his axe into its neck. As another ran to join its comrades that surrounded Esian it scratched deep into Orik's back knocking him to the ground. Esian was now surrounded by the remaining four Skanes. There was a pause as they all snarled and shrieked at him. Esian attacked breaking the leg of one of them with a kick to the knee. Ebonyr jumped on its back and slit its throat. As another lunged for Esian knocking Ebonyr flying with the back of its fist. Esian dropped his bow

and drew his swords stabbing and slashing wildly he thought he had dispatched of the last the three but slowly a Skane with a deep laceration that was pouring with blood rose behind him. He did not notice. Orik with his last ounce of strength before he could no longer hold onto his consciousness threw his mighty axe. Esian seeing this thinking his friend had gone mad rolled out of the way as it buried its self directly in the middle of the beasts face.
"Esian!" Ebonyr shouted as Orik lost consciousness.

Orik's eyes opened with fear. Baring down on him were the blooded soaked faces of Esian and Ebonyr.
"How long," he said. "Don't worry my friend we are safe for the time being. You have been asleep for only a few hours however you were hurt in the battle your back got slashed"
"Well its ok Ebonyr you can use that stuff you used on Esian, cant you?"
"I am afraid that was the last I had. I am afraid you will have to deal with the pain but I did manage to stop the bleeding" Orik huffed as he struggled to get to his feet.
"I do owe you my thanks though Orik"
"It is ok Ebonyr there is no need I just hope that you would do the same for me" the both shared a nod of the head and carried on. They could not move as fast as they could before as Orik's pace was a lot slower the sun began to rise and Ebonyr did not notice she glanced towards the sun almost instantly she dropped to the floor screaming in pain.
"What it is?" Esian shouted the screams got louder and louder.
"What?" shouted Orik only two words could be distinguished in the pain addled screams.
"My feather" Orik and Esian searched her person but it could not be found. Orik remembered that he had seen her put it down the front of her undergarments, not even thinking he grabbed it and clipped it to her ear. His face met with an

almighty slap from Ebonyr.

"That is for not asking permission" Orik's face dropped as he looked to Esian

"Can't win" Esian chuckled as did Orik but still they could not understand what just happened.

"What was that about," Esian asked while walking after Ebonyr who looked like she was trying to escape.

"My eyes, I see everything. I don't see shapes as you see them but emotion. Fear, excitement, love anything you can think of. They look like how you would see smoke drifting in the wind, always moving. But it comes with a price because the light heightens this ability and the pain is unbearable it freezes your whole body. But in the dark, it's wonderful the relief is bliss" it was clear to Ebonyr that they did not completely understand what she was and that Liniechs where all but unknown to the people of this age.

"Tracks!" Esian shouted the three toes of a Skane could be seen clearly in the dirt. "We must be close" Esian picked up the pace focused on the retrieval of his mother's necklace.

"I canny keep up with you laddy"

"Then go home!" Esian stopped as Orik's face turned sour "Orik I didn't me....." his sentence was interrupted by Orik pushing past him walking ahead Orik did not like how his friend was acting of late he thought it odd it was not like him to act like this. Ever since Ebonyr entered their company he had been acting this way. Ebonyr stayed silent for the most of the day.

"What was that the skane stole from you also Ebonyr?" Orik enquired trying to find out who she actually was "and why are you not in your mountains?"

"If you must know I am the high priestess of my people. The one who can see all and also the only one who feels the pain I feel. I begged for help from my kin but received none so I ran; I deserted my own people in search of a way to rid me of this pain. But I have not yet found a way" Ebonyr did not want to tell the others what she had actually found out as she did not think it wise if she had told them that the last high priestess was, in fact, Esian's mother and the object Ebonyr sought was her necklace then she didn't think she would be in their company much longer.

"I cannot go much longer I am in too much pain and my bones are older than yours I need rest"

"So do we all my friend" the sleepless nights were taking their toll on them all as it was only mid-afternoon but to them, it felt like the middle of the night. They made a camp right where they were Esian thought it was not wise to make a fire because although the forest was dense a fire could be seen through it and especially as he thought they might be close to the Skanes they were seeking. As Esian took off his armour Orik caught sight of a small Skane bite on his upper left arm he thought this could be an explanation for his strange behavior as some Skane bite have some sort of venom in them there has only been one other case of it in the history of Areien but it was way before Orik was born.

In the middle of the night Orik awoke to relieve himself as he stood up he something moved in the shadows, he grabbed the first weapon to hand that happened to be Esians sword. Edging forward the shadow got closer, his breathing quickened. Out of the shadows walked a small dwarf the face of which Orik recognized it was Darek. His arms were cut and the shield that he carried was splintered, his hands battered and bruised.

"What are you doing here?" Orik's words seemed to echo in the night

"We were attacked on the road to new town, they ....killed Kien"

"Who did?" Orik asked knowing full well what the answer would be.

"Skanes, they were organized the same ones that attacked my village I heard of your quest when I got to new town and spoke with Vigor he mentioned the man and you but not the woman?" he said noticing Ebonyr laying with Esian. "Who is she?"
"I shall explain in the morning my friend first, rest"

Darek woke to Esian's arrow pressed up against his forehead.
"You move you die!" Orik woke up and immediately lunged for Esian.
"He is with us Esian, he is my friend" Orik grabbed Esian's arm and lowered it.
"Esian may I introduce you to Darek the newest member of our company"
"What is his skill?"
"His skill is....actually what is your skill"
"I have none to speak of I just want to avenge my wife"
"That's good enough for me but it is not safe do not expect to have an easy journey"
"Right let's get some breakfast" Esian went out into the wilderness he did not take his armour or weapons just his bow and arrows. He stayed low to the ground skulking in the long grass he kept a watchful eye on his surroundings and looked around for breakfast to show itself. By chance a deer wandered by about 40 feet in front of him he stepped forward to take his stance cracking a branch as he did so the deer bolted so Esian fired his arrow and pierced it through the heart. He carried it back to the camp and gave it to Orik to prepare

"Well Orik I must say that was delicious," Darek said with agreement from the others they all packed up their things and moved on following the tracks of the skane they hope so desperately to find before they come across any more trouble.
"So how is it you know Orik," Esian asked Darek

"I only know him through tragic circumstances. Your friend is a hero, after my village was attacked by a group of Skanes Orik stumbled upon it by chance he could have just carried on walking but he saw a dying child lying in the dirt, he did not know the child he could have just walked on but he stopped and did everything he could to keep him alive. He walked into what was left of my house and search for aid me and my wife hid like cowards and did not help our kin but Orik sought us out and pleaded with us for aid. Sadly the child did not survive but I think Orik still keeps him alive" Esian looked at Orik with admiration and respect but this was short lived as he saw his friend shot through the head with an arrow from a direction which he did not know it came from nowhere and obliterated his skull.

"Are you okay?" Orik asked Esian
"Orik? I-I I just saw you….."
"Esian come on laddy we have a long walk ahead of us" the fog started to settle again like a blanket of snow on the ground the forest became less dense and the company could see further ahead than before in the distance they could see a small house that was mixed with the wilderness it twisted and turned around the trees as the threes. Made of wood it flowed through the forest it was almost as if it was one with the forest and it looked like it had been there for a good long while for moss was calling it home and branches delved in and out of its crevasses.
"Let me go first," Ebonyr said she walked up to the porch of the house and took off her raven feathers. Tensing every muscle in her body to make sure she didn't scream. She took an intake of breath before she opened her eyes. She took a moment to look inside the house and at the surroundings.
"There is nobody here," she said as she shielded her eyes with the raven feathers once more. They all went into the house walking slowly. The wood moaned beneath their feet.

The house was small made of one room. A table with 5 chairs sat in the middle with a fire at one end and a small kitchen at the other and a bed lay in the corner.

"Finally somewhere comfortable to sit down," said Orik walking with a brisk pace he sat down in the chair wincing as he forgot the wound on his back as it pressed up against the backrest. They all sat around the table to have a rest. They just started to have a decent conversation about what they should do next when footsteps came from outside and the withered humming of an old man.

"Hide" Esian whispered. The others obey instantly fearing what would happen if a crazy hermit found them in his house. The old man walked in.

"I know you are here dwarfs man and Liniech I have been waiting for you" astonished, they all came out of their hiding places. Orik and Darek came from two cupboards in the kitchen; Esian and Ebonyr came from under the bed. The old man was dressed in dirty brown robes that had obviously been in contact with the mud and it had bits of broken twigs and branches intertwined with its thread.

"Who are you?" asked Darek

"Me? Who are you master dwarf"

"Answer his question old man," said Esian whilst drawing an arrow. The old man, muttered something under his breath, as he did so Esian's bow was flung to the other side of the room. They all recoiled in shock.

"The wizard of the forest," said Orik as he dropped to one knee to bow.

"Please, there is no need to bow. I have been watching your quest from afar I can tell you that all you fear is correct someone is organizing the Skanes but I am afraid I cannot tell who or what. But what I can tell you is that your mother necklace is more important that you know"

"What do you mean?" asked Esian

"Why don't you ask your Liniech friend?" they all turned to

Ebonyr.

"What does he mean lass?"

"I don't know" she snapped. Ebonyr walked out of the house into the forest. Darek and Esian walked after her.

"What did you mean by that?" Orik asked the old man.

"It is not my place to say master dwarf"

"Orik get out here!" Orik ran out the door to be met by 5 Skanes two of which were holding Ebonyr by her arms.

"Darek here!" Orik threw one of his swords to Darek; he fumbled as he caught it. As he regained his balance he managed to swipe the sword at the skane that was running towards him. He sliced its shoulder making it fall to the side Orik ran towards the two that where remaining, an arrow flew past his head and obliterated the skull of one of them. Orik jumped in the air swinging his axe as he came down to the ground he flung it into the chest of the other. The two Skanes bolted into the forest carrying Ebonyr on their backs. Esian, Orik, and Darek ran after them dodging the protruding roots and the branches that grabbed at them. The Skanes soon disappeared from sight. They kept running in the same direction soon they came to a clearing that was occupied by a large camp. Wooden walls laid out in a circle with a small break that acted as a gate, they were sharpened to a point at the top. Small huts laid inside the perimeter and a small fire ablaze in the middle. They all hid in the bushes. Skane centuries patrolled the outer and inner perimeter. They wore armour on the body legs and head. It was black with sharp spikes flying backward from the shoulders and the calves. It had strange markings that cover the armour.

"I bet that's where they are keeping her" Esian whispered

"They are so organized," Orik said in a surprised tone. His surprise was very justified as Skanes would never normally hunt in packs in most cases if a Skane stood in the way of another, it would not hesitate to rip it limb from limb. They did not approve of working together.

"Should we attack?" asked Darek
"No laddy, that would not be wise, 5 Skanes is one thing 40 is another"
"What about the wizard surely he would help us?"
"No, he does not interfere with the issues of others" the three of them agreed to go back to the wizards house to ask for food and shelter as they turned to crawl away without being seen. They heard a warble screech come from the camp they looked around and they could see a warble facing up to Kane ranks many Skanes jumped on it ripping its skin off with their claws it tried to fight them off but they were too many soon it was dismembered and carried into the camp, the Skanes jumping and shrieking, carrying it above their heads like a trophy. They had never eaten warble before. Orik, Esian, and Darek went back to the wizard's house. Shuddering at what they had just seen.

Ebonyr's hands were bound above her head, strapped to a post they started to ache through her raven feathers she could make out the shape of a dwarf. He ripped her mask off and threw it on the fire. She screamed an almighty scream as the dwarf male recoiled in horror he noticed her eyes.
"You fools!" he shouted "you have captured a Liniech. How did this bunch of rabble catch you?" his question was ill received and Ebonyr spat on his face in retaliation the dwarf lifted a burning bit of wood from the fire and put it close to her eyes making the pain more intense, another scream leaked from her lips as black tear dropped from her eyes. The dwarf leant into Ebonyr and whispered in her ear.
"I will break you Linieh"
"You can try!"

As they got to the house they could hear the pain addled screams from the camp they knew exactly what was happening. The wizard was waiting for them at the door.

"Come in," he said "if you are hungry I will feed you if you are tired I will provide a place to rest" they all thanked him and scuttled inside, waiting for them on the table was a feast of every type of meat and ale sat beside every plate. Their stomachs had been yearning for a good meal for a long time. They all sat and scoffed their faces they were all nearly done by the time the wizard had taken but only his first bite.

"Is there anymore?" Orik requested only to receive a kick from Esian

"It's quite alright said the wizard there is more in the kitchen" Orik shot to his feet as did Darek and they filled their plates once more.

"So what are you going to do about your Liniech?"

"I do not know we cannot beat them when we number only three there is no way we can sneak her out of there I have no idea what to do"

"Skanes are reptilian," said Darek "so they have no energy in the night time because they have no sun to heat their blood"

"So…." Said Orik

"So we can attack them at night when they are all asleep, the sleep as if they were dead and the ones that aren't asleep cannot move as normal we would be able to dispatch of them quickly enough"

"Very good master dwarf," said the wizard "that is the only way I can see that you will succeed and you only have an hour or two before dark"

"That settles it we shall go an hour after dark," said Orik

"Esian..."

Esian was staring at the door as an overwhelming sense of fear came over him as a Skane burst through the door he looked around the table at his friends to find that they were also Skanes

"What devilry is this!" he drew his sword and swung it at what used to be Orik only to be blasted back by a force that he could not see he landed in front of the fire and lost consciousness.

The wizard lifted Esian's eyes and it was completely blacked out as if it was one large pupil.
"This man has received a bite from a venomous Skane, he will be dead by morning unless you can get me the venom from the same Skane and I will be able to make an anti-venom"
"But how do we tell which one has venom"
"Their scales are slightly darker than the others and their front teeth longer, take this with you," the wizard said while handing them a vial. The night closed in around them and it was time if they succeeded they could save both their friends with one swoop.

Orik took off his armour so his steps would be silent he took only his knife that sat in his boot and his sword. Darek still had the sword that Orik gave to him in the last fight. They left the house and walked toward the encampment. When they got there, there was only one guard patrolling the perimeter, Orik slowly slid the knife out of his pocket and threw it towards the Skane it flew through its eye and out the back of its skull sticking the wood behind it. Orik and Darek ran up to either side of the gate looking in to see what enemies they would have to fight. To their surprise, there wasn't many walking around. Orik looked desperately to find the venomous Skanes but could not see any. There was a large hut that sat in front of the fire he could see Ebonyr unconscious in front of it. They crept into the camp slitting the throat of any Skane standing. Still Silent like mice they made their way to Ebonyr. Orik then went and checked the huts looking for the venomous Skane but he could not find it. Fear crept up on his heart as he knew he was going to have to look in the main hut. He parted the curtain that acted as the door to find on one side a dwarf laying face down in bed and on the other the venomous Skane sleeping silently. Orik crept up to the side it. He did not know how to do this silently enough so he swung his sword and decapitated it as it slept on the ground. He did not make much noise but enough to make the dwarf toss in his sleep Orik daren't turn around so he walked out of the hut and put the vial up to the teeth of the dismembered Skane head and pushed. Venom filled the vial it had a thick consistency and it shone in the moonlight. Darek and Orik lifted Ebonyr from her bounds and carried her to the wizard's house.

As Orik walked in the door he handed the vial of venom to the wizard. He went and added it to a pot that was cooking in the kitchen, it sizzled and spat.
"Wake up lass". Orik said shaking the Liniech priestess.
She tossed and turned wincing with every move. Her body was cut and bruised. Ebonyr's eyes slowly opened causing intense pain The light of the house was too. Orik ripped off one of his sleeves and wrapped it around her like a blindfold.
"Thank you Orik," she said thankfully. "Where is Esian?"
The wizard bent over Esian and flooded his throat with the anti-venom he had created, hoping some would be swallowed. All of the green velvety liquid seeped down his throat until it was all gone.
"He will not wake for at least a day or if it has not worked he will be dead in the morning. Only time will tell. Now I think you should take this chance to rest". The old wizard went to every wall of the house chanting some sort of spell. Orik watched waiting to see if something amazing would happen but his hopes were dashed as nothing happened.
"What is your name, old man?"
"My name? My name has not been heard by anyone for a good two centuries. Do you know I have quite forgotten it myself." The wizard went and took some blankets and other comfortable things to sleep on and put them on the floor around the table.
"There you go, I know it's not much but I don't have any spare

beds lying around." Ebonyr was the first to take a space on the ground and fall asleep. The two dwarves stayed up talking of the perils that they may face and Orik explained how they came across Ebonyr.
"I don't entirely trust her," he said "I don't know why there is just something about her that seems, shifty"
The conversation soon became thin and they fell asleep on the cushions and blankets on the ground.

Orik was the first to awake darting to his friend's bedside to check that he was alive; an old cracked, raspy voice came from a chair in the corner.
"He is alive master dwarf don't you worry."
"Thank god I don't know where I would be without him, oh wait yes I do, back at home enjoying a nice pint of cutthroat."
"Well, I have a couple of pints worth of cutthroat here if you wish to take some."
"Yes thank you very much." Excitement took over his body as he sat on one of the dining chairs as the pint was put in front of him. He lifted up the tankard and as the golden ale graced his lips, he lent back, closed his eyes and enjoyed the immense bliss that was a cutthroat ale.
"Nice?" Asked the wizard. Orik raised his eyebrows in agreement but did not stop drinking, within a minute the last of the ale trickled down his throat bringing joy to his eyes where joy had been lost for a long time. It had been a long time since Orik could enjoy a carefree pint of cutthroat. Ebonyr woke drawing her dagger in anger.
"Bad dream?" Orik said with a sarcastic grin. She shot him a look of disapproval. As she walked outside to go the toilet she tripped over Darek and hit her head on the ground. Darek woke very disorientated. He stood up and looked around for a minute noticing all the branches that contorted around the wooden support beams of the house swirling down like constrictor snakes killing their prey. He paused for a second

looking around the room to get his bearings. The house seemed to be one with nature, it was beautiful.

"Ah Orik, what is the plan today?"

"We wait here until Esian is well and rested." Darek nodded. Ebonyr walked out of the house huffing and puffing as she left. Orik sat thinking about when he awoke alone in the small village on the way to New Town.

"So where were you?" Orik asked wanting to know why Darek and Kien left him in their house by himself.

"I am sorry Orik we couldn't bear sleeping in that house so we left for new town, but we got lost"

"So you left me on my own for the whole night…!"

"It matters not, you are all okay now." interrupted the wizard

"My wife is dead how is she ok?"

"I am sorry Darek," said Orik

"AH!" shouted the wizard

"What?" The dwarves replied

"I have remembered my name"

"Well?" They enquired.

"My name is Ethesir"

"Nice to meet you Ethesir," Darek shouted getting ahead of himself. Ebonyr walked back into the house.

"Ebonyr his name is Ethesir."

"Ethesir." She said with wide eyes "your name is legend."

"Thank you. As are your people, as are you, priestess."

"I do wish some of you would shut up. I am trying to sleep."They all span round to see the annoyed face of the man in their company.

"Esian bless you your awake," Ebonyr said as she ran to his side.

"What happened?" he asked.

"You where bitten my friend, by a skane."

"A skane I don't remember being bitten I only just remember waking up here" It is ok my friend you haven't missed anything exciting.

"We need to go after that skane I want my mother's necklace now!"

"In time my friend but first you need to rest." Esian frowned he approved of sitting around doing nothing.

"I'm just going to go and have a look around," he said.

"Be careful," replied Darek. Orik turned to leave looking back at Esian one last time just before he crossed the door to the outside. He noticed that Ebonyr had taken hold of his hand. When Orik got outside the light of the sun was bright. It left an imprint on the back of his eyes. He wandered through the bushes and past the trees, a foul smell lingered in the air. He saw smoke rising in the distance and a distorted light flickered through the trees. As Orik Crept closer he could see that the pack members camp had piled the carcasses of their dead, that Orik and Darek had killed the night before.as the last Skane left he put a torch to the pile setting ablaze. The stench was horrific and nearly unbearable. Just as Orik caught sight of the Dwarven leader, he turned his back and walked into the camp clenching his fist around what looked like the chain of a necklace. Orik ran back to the wizard's house hoping to find his friends, as he approached he could see the warm orange glow of flames, as he moved closer to the house he saw it was ablaze, six men were walking away from it laughing and jesting with each other. Orik hid in the bushes watching their every move. As he watched they walked into the tree line, if he looked hard enough he could see a group of shadows moving in the cover of the forest. They were moving fast with little sound. Soon they were out of sight but the fact they intentionally burnt down Ethesir's house meant they knew exactly what they were doing.

Chapter V
A Sinister Plot

In the night air, a group of six men sat around a campfire. They all talked as they drank ale and feasted on deer that had been caught only an hour before.
"Ha that pathetic Liniech and her friends never knew what was coming to her," said one with a harsh but jolly voice.
"Well she did or it wouldn't have been empty when we got there now, would it? How could they have known we were tracking them." Said another. They all wore green and brown leathers, each man had a bow and quiver placed next to him no other weapons were in sight. They all wore hoods that covered their faces. The brown leather boots were worn on their feet. The only metal they had was on their belt buckles, which were all a different shape and style, and they each had a ring on the same finger and each other the designs mirrored the belt buckles. Firlorn who was the leader of the group was the only one to have a beard. He had long black hair that fell just below his ears and had a fringe the stayed above his eyebrows. his belt buckle was a large golden dragon wound in a circle around itself and his ring matched. The dragon was decorated with an emerald eye.

As they slept that night they each took it in turns to watch the surroundings. They were lucky on this night as no real danger presented its self. In the morning they woke and had the left over's from dinner the night before for breakfast.
"You will need your strength, my brothers. Eat up" they all obeyed without question.
"So where do you suppose they went Firlorn?" Asked one of

the men. He was clean-shaven, tall with blonde hair that did not stretch far from his head. His skin was scared with multiple lacerations and burn marks. His belt buckle was plain and silver but had an engraving on the top that read 'fear the merciless.' He had this engraving because he believed he was merciless. So he felt that as long as he had that engraving everyone would fear him. Needless to say, he was not the smartest of the group.
"I don't know Lomak but I intend to find out" the group of men were organized in a line as they walked through the dense forest.
"There." The man at the front whispered.
"Up into the trees," said Firlorn. The men scarpered up into the trees holding themselves over a path that a group of Skanes where taking. As they past Firlorn counted them. Six had passed them. He nodded to his company signalling to attack. They all took out their bows. Lomak fumbling around to grab his bow that he had put awkwardly around his back, fell to the floor with a thud making a loud noise. As the Skanes turned round the others took aim. All of them marked a different target to the others. Firlorn gave the signal to fire 5 arrows flew through the air killing every target that they were meant for. Just as the last skane reached Lomak the largest of the men, Krigor jumped from the branch on which he sat, wielding an arrow in one hand. As he flew through the air he knocked it in his bow and fired it, it ripped through the neck of the skane that was now bent over Lomak, stopping just a centimeter before making contact with Lomak's face. As Krigor landed next to him, Lomak pushed the Skane's body away and got to his feet spitting out the skane blood he now tasted.
"Thank you, my friend."
"Don't mention it." Krigor didn't wear a long-sleeved shirt like the rest of his kin for his muscles would burst right out of it, the veins that ran down his arm looked like the roots of the very forest in which he walked. He had short brown hair that was

always messy.

"How many times have I told you to not put your bow on that way. Remember sling it over one shoulder that way it is easy to grab in a hurry"

"I know Firlorn I'm sorry."

"Firlorn look at this," said Krigor as he turned the body of a dead skane. "These have the same mark as the ones we saw in the camp yesterday. A dwarven anvil in a circle with spikes around the outside."

"Very curious. But we cannot get distracted from our goal. We must find the Liniech."

"I cannot wait to rip out that priestess' eyes. The gold is going to plentiful" said Krigor.

"Yes, Krigor, what do you intend to do with your share."

"Intend to buy a house in New Town."

"The sounds nice but we are not allowed. Are we?" asked Lomak rhetorically

"No, we are not but with the amount that I am going to offer. They won't be able to refuse and then I get to irritate all the dwarves and scare all of the traitors."

"That is a good plan my friend," said Firlorn. "I myself want to go out into the country and build a small cabin by the waterside for my family and me."

"When did Firlorn here become a female." laughing as he said this Krigor slapped Firlorn on the back.

"I could still best you in any fight on any day in any weather my friend," he replied.

They stopped and sat down for food.

"Where's Riorc?" said Lomak the others shot up shouting his name looking through the trees and scouring the landscape.

"Weapons!" shouted Firlorn. They all drew their bows and knocked arrows in them. They backtracked their steps in hope to find him all the while shouting his name. Shadows moved beneath the trees. The whisper of malice echoed in the trees.

Firlorn noticed shade bile on the leaves of a nearby bush; a shade spreads this bile around when they are the prey as it neutralizes their stench and makes them undetectable...

"Shades!" he said, "keep your eyes open." As he said this even the slightest sound that was caught by the men made them jump and snap their heads to its origin. Suddenly another man, Fleck was nowhere to be seen. Retches could be heard not far away, the four remaining men darted for it and there, in a small clearing four shades in a square with the two men on their knees in the middle. Shades where strange being purple in color but they were not exactly solid beings although they choose to be corporeal if they wished, in the no corporeal form their whole body was made of smoke making them impossible to kill. Their face was non-existent other than a few holes in the cloud. The smell of the mist was not pleasant it made the eyes of the men water. Out of nowhere a flaming arrow burst out of the trees and landed next to one of the shadows it let out a scream and fled into the trees disappearing as it did so. The other four searched the area. A dwarf appeared out of the tree line running directly past the shades to the men giving them wood that was ablaze, seeing this one the shades flew through Riorc pulling out his heart on the way through.

"NO!" shouted Firlorn running towards the shade with the wood in his hand, Fleck rolled making a step for Firlorn, he pushed off of his back with his foot flying over the shade throwing the flaming wood into the head of the shade making the smoke disappear. Lomak fired an arrow behind fleck. Fleck then dug the arrow out of the ground and using its sharp edges freed himself. A shade took its physical form giving the dwarf an opportunity to kill it, he spun around throwing his axe with an almighty fury. The shade let it phase through it causing no damage it became solid again spawning a sword from its hand and ran towards the dwarf. He drew his sword, as Fleck evaded the attacks of the shade he noticed the engraving in

the axe buried in the ground. The shade swung his sword at the dwarf, ducking he stabbed the leg of the evil beast. An arrow came from across the clearing hitting the hand of the shade making it drop the sword. As it hit the ground it disappeared. Lomak and Krigor ran up behind it kicking it to the floor and then shot an arrow each into the back of its head. It too disappeared when it hit the floor. They all turned and stared at the last shade and with a poof, it was gone.
"Thank you master dwarf for an old man you are skilled we are in your debt," said Firlorn.
"His name is Orik said, Fleck."
"You read dwarven," said Orik. Yanking his axe from the ground
"A little."
"Well, Orik I am pleased you showed up who knows what would have happened."
"What are we going to do about Riorc," said Fleck.
"We must bury him," replied Lomak.
"We do not have time my friend's darkness is nearly upon us, Riorc would understand," said Firlorn. "You are welcome to join us Orik if you wish."
"Firlorn! Is that wise, he is a dwarf."
"I know Krigor but he saved our lives and the least you could do is show a little gratitude, so Orik are you with us?"
"Yes, but I might inquire what you young lads are doing in the forest."
"We are tracking a group of people we believe they have something of ours." Firlorn's deception was obvious to Orik but he did not show it.
"Do you know who?"
"No, only that there is a man a dwarf and a Liniech and a wizard also." Orik nodded along giving no hint that he knew who he was on about, he was on edge and did not trust these men by any degree.

Chapter VI
A Lone Dwarf

"You must believe me a group of men are coming for Ebonyr." said Ethesir "We must leave or we will all perish." Esian, Darek, Ebonyr, and Ethesir all ran out of the house and into the woods
"What about Orik?" said Esian
"Orik has a larger part to play in this part of your quest; he will be fine on his own."
"He is a dwarf," Darek added as they ran through the forest they could hear the cracking of Ethesir's house being reduced to ash.
"Ebonyr is anything following us?" asked Esian.
She whipped around taking off her blindfold.
"No, we are safe for now."
"Who is chasing us and why are they chasing us."
"That I do not know and cannot answer I just know that it is a group of men that want us for a reason I cannot see. We cannot remain here they may discover us."
"Well, then what kind of wizard are you?" Shouted Ebonyr
Esian looked at her with angry eyes.
"That was uncalled for," he said. Suddenly they heard noises in the darkness this spurred them to walk on until morning. Esian thought of his friend he was worried about what may have happened to him maybe the men had captured him he thought. As his emotions swelled inside him he busied himself with other things to keep his mind off his worries.
"Stop." Ebonyr whispered, "look." She pointed out a large skane patrol walking only a few meters ahead of them. They were all in ranks but in the middle of them was a dwarf astride a jet black pony. He was wearing the necklace around his

neck; it caught the light of the moon and a glint of light shot into Esian's and Ebonyr's eyes.
"The necklace." they both whispered. Esian looked at Ebonyr.

"What did you say?"
"I said nothing."
"You recognized my mother's necklace how and why do you want it?"
"I don't know what you are talking about." Esian drew an arrow and pointed it at Ebonyr making the arrowhead touch her nose.
"You will tell me."
"Esian!" shouted Darek. "Enough."
"Ok I'll tell you." submitted Ebonyr. "First of all, you must know that your mother was a Liniech. In fact, she was my predecessor."
"You lie my mother was human she did not have your eyes or the pain you endure when opening them."
"No your mother could not bear the pain that ailed her, none of the others would understand so she ran, she ran as far as she could. When she arrived New Town she looked for a way to end her suffering and she did. She was told of a necklace, a necklace that was lost centuries ago and this necklace had the power to turn any Liniech human, with the right incantation. She looked everywhere for it. When by chance she stumble upon it at a market going for only two silver pieces. Twenty years later you were born. Now I seek the same thing, unfortunately, it also has another function with the opposite incantation it has the power to control every Liniech in Areien and now he has it."
"I do not believe you. My mother was human. Why are you lying, you lied to us before. So why would I believe you now"
"I am sorry Esian but she is telling the truth, now lower you bow" Esian's bow lowered Ethesir went on to describe how he

had heard such tales before.

Esian's thoughts turned to his mother and found himself being angry. He was angry as he felt that his whole life had been a lie. How she could have done that to her own son. He separated himself from the group for a while and walked to the bank of the river. He took off his boots and dangled his feet in the water. The refreshing cold seemed to calm his mood. On the opposite side of the river he could see the army of Skanes, moving swiftly he hid. In the middle of the skane ranks, he could see the dwarf and in turn his mother's necklace. He slowly and silently drew an arrow from his quiver; calmly he drew his bow and aimed at the head of the mounted dwarf. He took up the slack. Just before he was about to fire. He saw the profile of a dwarf he knew so well following behind them, hiding in the shadows. Esian knew then if he released his arrow the enemy could be alerted to the presence of Orik. He was happy to know that his friend was alive and not captured by the enemy. Esian stayed still and made no sound; he watched his friend until he went out of sight. He didn't have to wait for long as the skane army turned and disappeared into the tree line. Esian knew he could not catch up with them in time. The bridge to the other side of the river was too far away. But he could not understand why the Skanes where leaving their camp. It looked like they were heading to New Town. If this was, in fact, the truth it would be a dark day for all.

Ebonyr looked around for Esian but did not want to leave the group. They discussed the possibility of heading back to New Town, maybe Orik is waiting for them there. The full moon had reached its highest point and Ethesir was all but asleep. Esian walked through the trees bearing two rabbits in his hand. The excitement grew on Darek's face looking forward to some actual food once again. Ebonyr sat next to Esian. He moved to the other side of Darek avoiding all contact with Ebonyr, even though he hated her for lying to him. He could not hate her outright. There was something in his gut telling him he should not have moved but he was not going to let his emotions get the better of him. Darek roasted the rabbits over the fire lightly seasoning them with herbs that he found about the small clearing. Darek ate a whole rabbit to himself. Reluctantly Esian cut his in half and gave it to Ebonyr as he passed it their hands connected. Esian felt as if lightning bolts shot up his arm but in actual fact, it was all in his imagination he pulled his arm away with force, after finishing his meal, he went straight to sleep.

Esian woke up first. He walked to a tree which he recognized as a Bloodheart tree. It was called this because of the beautiful red leaves it would produce in a most elegant shape, they were mostly used as a gift a groom would give to his bride before the wedding, but Esian spotted one leaf that had grown in the perfect shape to cover Ebonyr's eyes. He plucked it from the tree delicately bending the stalk into a hook that would fit her ear he left it next to her as she slept. While he was waiting for the others to wake. He thought he would sit down and enjoy a nice smoke on his pipe. Darek woke with a mighty belch that erupted from his stomach. He looked at Esian and they both laughed knowing that they would have to laugh at the little things. Ebonyr awoke reaching for her blindfold but picked up the Bloodheart leaf instead she hooked in on her ear and looked at Esian.
"Thank you very much, my friend." Esian nodded in agreement understanding her gratitude. An hour past and the sun was beating down on them. Esian feeling the boredom take over him walked over to Ethesir and kicked him awake.
"How dare you kick me." his voice seemed to shake the very ground which they all stood. Squirrels and mice all scuttled away. Ethesir noticing that the sun was up soon calmed down

and apologized. Esian told the group of what he had seen the night before and the fact that he saw Orik in pursuit of the Skane army.

"I don't think they will risk going to new town just yet it is too dangerous for them."

"I don't think their destination is New Town, I think it is the Barrow Mountains, my home." said Ebonyr "They will be scouring the forest for any last recruits."

"Now that is a troubling thought," said Darek.

"We should go to New Town and ask them for aid." They all agreed. If the dwarf leader could control the Liniech's then he could wage an almighty war on Areien. It was half a days walk to the bridge as they got to the other side of the river they saw four shades drifting through the wilderness. All of their thoughts where with Orik now. What if these shades found Orik he would have no chance alone. This put them all in a state of dread. They all followed the Shades to make sure they did not find Orik. luckily they were not downwind of these foul creatures. Suddenly they disbursed. They were no were to be seen.

"Ebonyr anything?" Esian whispered.

"Nothing." suddenly in the distance they could hear the retching of the shades. They ran to the origin of the sound. To find a standoff between a group of men and four shades. All of them looked at each other and they all knew what the other was thinking. If they were to stay put maybe the group of men would be eradicated. All of sudden a flaming arrow burst out of the trees and landed next to one of the shades, it let out a scream and fled into the tree line disappearing as it did so. A dwarf ran out of the tree line and sprinted past the shades.

"Orik," Esian said as he got up to go and help his friend. Ethesir grabbed his arm keep him in place.

"Wait." He whispered. "You will see." Ethesir holding complete confidence that Orik can hold is own all of a sudden a grief-ridden scream came from one of the men.

"NO!" the group were unaware why he did this until they altered their gaze and saw a shade drop the heart of one of the men as he fell to his knees.

"We must help Orik," said Darek.

"Wait," replied Ethesir. "He will be fine." as he said this they saw one of the men dodging a shade attack like an elf. He was so agile never before has a man been witnessed being this agile. It was like he was one with air and the air carried him. The shades would attack and he would seem to merely drift out of their way. He made it look effortless. At one point he rolled close to where Orik's axe had been thrown to the ground he looked directly at them but did not see them. When the battle had drawn to a close Orik collected his axe. He bent down to lift it from the grip of the earth. He turned his head to the group, completely closed one eye and smirked.

"You read dwarven," he said as he walked away.

"What do we do know," Esian asked the wizard.

"We follow them, we learn what they want and we learn how to get our Orik back." they all agreed to follow the group of men.

Chapter VII
Unexpected allies

"Why does that one not talk?" asked Orik.
"Who Sureck? He can't he doesn't have a tongue. It was cut out when he was taken prisoner by your kind." replied Krigor spitefully.
"Krigor that's enough," said Firlorn. The road ahead looked sullen even in the beautiful light of dusk it was hostile.
The trees loomed overhead, they looked evil in the oncoming darkness. The slender branched seemed to grab their extremities. They accentuate every shadow making the very bravest of warriors shake in their boots. Lomak hesitated before journeying into this part of the forest.
"They are just trees," said Fleck. He walked backward hitting into a branch protruding from a tree letting out a shriek as he did so. Lomak laughed and he felt a little more comfortable walking through this scary part of the forest.

The mist of Nosver soon set in ever so discreetly. It kept them from seeing further than a few feet in front of them. By chance, Orik was at the back of the group he was minding his own business making sure he could still see Fleck in front of him. When a hand clasped his mouth and ripped him into the void. He drew his knife from his boot and stabbed the thigh of his assailant.
"Ah Orik it's me," said a familiar voice. Orik turned round to see that he had attacked and injured Darek.
"Darek my friend I am sorry lad but you should have identified yourself sooner." He fell to the floor with a thud. Ethesir, Ebonyr, and Esian came through the mist revealing

themselves. Ethesir put his hands over Darek's wound and whispered some ancient language. Before their very eyes, the valley of his laceration closed and the blood dried, he was fixed. The others could not believe their eyes bewildered by the speed in which the wound had healed. The conversation was soon changed and directed at Orik and his involvement with the men.

"Orik what are you doing with them. They are hunting us," said Esian who was confused why Orik was staying with them but also he was elated to see his friend again. He could not help but walk up to him and hold him in a harsh embrace.

"If I am with them I can find out what they want," Orik said. Ethesir looked at Orik in admiration nodding along with his plan.

Orik walked back and joined the group of men, Fleck did notice his absence.

"So what is it that these people took from you Firlorn?" asked Orik.

"You are not yet known well enough for us to divulge that information to you," said Krigor.

"Krigor this dwarf saved our lives. If he is to be with us he must know our plan. We are looking for the group because of the Liniech. Do you know what a Liniech's eyes look like?"

"I have heard…stories," Orik replied with no sign of deception.

"Well, I shall educate you more. They are like glass pools that encase pure white clouds that are rushing in the wind and on the black markets of Mardian they fetch a wealthy price." Orik clearing his throat trying to hide his disgust at the very notion of taking someone's eyes said.

"Oh-oh well, then we better get to it." The group of men kept walking always moving forward looking for clues as to where the Liniech may be hiding. Unbeknown to them if they had just turned around and walked a couple of paces in the opposite direction they would find her very soon, however they kept their course going in the wrong direction.

Lomak grew more and more wary of the fog. The fact that he could not see anything frightened him more than anything. He had always feared the unknown ever since he was a boy and for this, his parents always preferred his brother. But when his brother died in the great war they didn't care much for Lomak so he ran away and found Firlorn who was strong, courageous, intuitive and he always gave Lomak a chance. And they have been inseparable ever since. The bond is in fact not that different from that of brothers.
"Firlorn is there any sign of the fog letting up?" he shouted to the front of the party.
"No Lomak I am afraid not we may have to sleep in this shroud." The thought of sleeping in this place did not sit well with Lomak at all.

Orik decided that he would sneak away when they finally made camp and the men were asleep. He would find the others and tell of the men's plan. The danger was apparent to him. He knew that if he was caught leaving the camp to give information to their enemy. He would be slaughtered instantly and he would have led them straight to Ebonyr and this troubled him greatly. His thoughts were interrupted by a scream from the front of the party. When they all reached the front of the group, they found Firlorn had fallen down a hidden hole and was now unconscious at the bottom of a very deep, very dark pit.
"Firlorn!" they all shouted instantly Krigor started to walk away from the hole trailing rope behind him soon after, Lomak and Sureck grabbed hold. In no time at all Fleck was wrapped up in it and was descending into the hole held up by Lomak Krigor and Sureck. Orik watched in amazement at the efficiency of the group and how professional they acted in a crisis. He ran over and grabbed hold of the rope taking some

of the strain off the others. Slowly but surely Fleck got to the bottom of the hole.

"How is he?" Lomak shouted down.

"unconscious," replied Fleck.

"Has he any injuries?" inquired Krigor.

"I don't think it is anything major" Fleck tired the rope around Firlorn and shouted for the others to pull him up. As Firlorn reached the top Orik glanced behind him. What he saw struck fear in his heart. Two dozen Skanes now surrounded them. He whispered to the others the all drew their bows and span around making a circle around Firlorn.

"Protect Firlorn!" Krigor shouted all of a sudden Orik was nowhere to be seen. He had run and left them alone to face the skane horde.

"I am afraid you are going to have to climb Fleck!" Krigor said. Fleck snapped two arrows in half; stuck them into the mud that was the walls of the hill and used them to hoist himself upwards towards the surface every so often the ground would slip and he would have to react fast to thrust an arrow back in, in order to save himself from a nasty fall. Krigor knocked three arrows in his bow.

"Will that work?" asked Lomak

"Well shall soon find out." He released them they flew through the air perfectly hitting the targets they were intended for. As they all braced for battle out of nowhere the roots of the trees burst out of the ground pulling some of the Skanes back down with them. Both sides froze not knowing what had caused this. All of a sudden Esian, Ebonyr, Darek, Orik, and Ethesir sprinted out of the mist. Ebonyr threw two knives into the throat of one skane making it fall to its knees as its dark blue blood squirted from its body leaving a small puddle. Esian shot an arrow through the eye of one. This shot was so mighty that I went straight through and pierced the heart of another. The group ran next to where the men were standing. The all exchanged a nod of acknowledgment. Feeling the adrenaline they all charged towards the enemy throwing axes and firing arrows as they did so. Getting closer they drew their axes and swords the men stuck with their bows and fired from afar. Darek stabbed a skane with his sword as Orik chopped its head off. Eight Skanes now remained.

Krigor looked back at his leader lying by the side of the hole in the ground. A skane was running for him he drew an arrow but just before he released it he saw Fleck's hands at the top of the hole. He pulled himself up with force making him fly in the air on his way down he pulled an arrow from his quiver and stabbed it into the chest of the skane that was about to kill Firlorn, he then fired an arrow past Krigor's left ear, missing it by millimeters, hitting a skane that was behind him. Firlorn regained consciousness, greeted by Fleck.

"We are under attack, quick!" Firlorn jumped to his feet and drawing his bow. He witnessed Sureck fighting a skane. Sureck stabbed it in the leg with an arrow, letting out a scream it hit him in the face leaving him dazed then it kicked him to his knees. It then looked at Firlorn as it dug its claws into the bottom of Sureck's chin and lifted its arm separating his head from his shoulders. All of the men witnessed this and they all ran straight for it. Fleck was the first to reach it he jumped evading an attack and wrapped his arms around its neck holding himself on its back. Krigor was next to get there slicing the back of its legs with a knife he found on the way. The skane screeched as it fell to its knees. Firlorn and Lomak reached it at the same time, simultaneously drew an arrow and walked right up to it shooting it in each eye. As they turned around they saw that the others had wiped out the rest of the horde.

"Orik what are you doing with them, and her," said Firlorn.

"They are my friends. They are also the only reason why you are still alive." The sound of branches breaking and skane screeches came from the trees. The horde had heard the slaughter and wanted revenge.

"You hear that?" said Esian. That is the sound of our immediate demise unless we go now!" The newly allied group ran in the direction they deemed most safe. Firlorn did not take his eyes off Ebonyr the whole time they were sprinting.

When they finally came to a stop Firlorn briskly walked up to Ebonyr snatching the knife from Krigor's hand. He pulled Ebonyr's perfect hair whipping her head back he put the knife to her neck. She raised one eyebrow with arrogance, Firlorn lowered his gaze Ebonyr's knife was pressed up against the inside of his legs.
"Don't even try," she whispered in his ear.
"Her eyes...." said Ethesir. The group looked at him "T-that's why they want her because of her eyes."
"You are intuitive, who are you?"
"He is Ethesir. He is the wizard of the forest and you will show him your respect."
"I need her eyes or my family dies!" The whole group, excluding the men, stood at arms.
"You dare and you die!" said Darek. The men drew their bows and pointed them at each individual.
"STOP!" said Orik. "This is stupid we should be working together to fight this scourge that lies upon the land not fighting each other. Or we might as well go home now and wait for the inevitable. All of us could do some real good if we just work together. We are fighters all of us and we can win this fight if we work hard enough. I'm not saying it's going to be easy but I have spent time with both of you now and I know that these men are not bad people. They are just fighting to survive, I know we can do it if we just try."
"I like the way you think Orik but how can we be expected to trust each other. After all our races were at war."
Silence fell, as weapons were lowered and minds were opened. Each individual thought of something different for Orik it was of home and his forge and his family, but he thought a

lot about his new found family. Esian thought about the trust he holds for Orik and whether this new group of men can really be trusted. Ebonyr thought of nothing else but killing each and every man she saw before her, not including Esian of course. She imagined the slow and painful deaths in which she could inflict on all of them. Firlorn could only think of the safety and well being of him and his men and hope that his doubts about the uneasy alliance would not be proved.

"Let's hunt some Skanes!" said Firlorn.
Eventually, after a long silence, the group decided to move off in search of the Skanes.
"Where are we going?" asked Orik.
"We are going deeper into Nosver," Firlorn replied.
Lomak gulped in fear, Orik walked up beside him and offered him a drink from his flask, patted him on the back.
"We will be fine me'lado."
"STOP!" screamed Ebonyr. "What are we doing these men just tried to kill me to sell my eyes and now we are just going to blindly trust them and put our lives in their hands."
"We have no other choice," said Esian.
"I have a choice." she turned and ran disappearing into the mist.
"Ebonyr wait," Orik shouted after her.
"#Let her go, lad, she is a Liniech she will go where the elements take her, she will be fine," said Ethesir. with a reassuring tone in his old crackled voice.

Chapter VIII
Alone

Ebonyr ran in a straight line, as time seemed to disappear, thoughts ran through her head, fears entered her very soul. She was lost now, lost in the dark abyss that is Nosver forest. Noises, so many noises echoing from all directions. Ebonyr drew her fighting knives and kept on running hoping she would soon come to the end of the forest but luck was not on her side, trees seemed to grab her as she moved and soon fatigue got the better of her. She fell to her knees and breathed heavily. Ebonyr could not run any further. Fear gripped her, she could not move. Ebonyr could barely catch her breath. She looked into the distance trying to see what lay before her. The darkness of the forest shrouded all things. Ebonyr gained the energy to ascend a tree. She thought at least if she is off the ground. It would be safer until morning. In the moment before sleep took her, she remembered Orik and Esian and how she hoped they were safe.
Morning came as swiftly as it left. The light shone through the trees and Ebonyr awoke. She gracefully dropped from the tree landing perfectly on her feet.

She did not know which way to go. She believed it had been only a couple of days since she left. The Liniech, fallen into her old ways and lost track of time. She decided to go north. She tried to use the sun to orientate herself but the canopy blocked out the sun. She did not want to climb the trees to find the sun as it would put her in pain but she had no choice. Halfway up out of the corner of her eye she saw what looked like the flick of a dwarven cloak. She ran across the tree-tops using every leaf and branch to her advantage. She stopped right above the head of the unsuspecting dwarf. She could see clearly now. The dwarf had the company of around 40 Skanes. She froze. Unaware of if her presence had gone unnoticed. She silenced her breath. She walked across the treetops keeping her eyes on the dwarf. He was rather tall, for a dwarf. Black hair that ran from his head to the bottom of his back he wore a cloak of skane skin and he wore an amulet. The crest upon the amulet was a silver circle with spiked edges and an anvil in the middle no hammer striking it or metal bent over it just an anvil. She knew now that this was the same dwarf that they were all hunting. Upon witnessing the amount of protection that this dwarf took with him she felt fear for the first time. She had never felt fear before. She didn't like it. Ebonyr composed herself shook off the fear as if it was water in her hair. She continued her pursuit until they came to a clearing in the trees. In the middle there was a camp huge in size and legions of Skanes resided there. In a small corner, there were cages of humans and dwarves alike sitting there crying looking outward with hope in their eyes. In the centre, Skanes with no mark walked up to a post where they braced themselves against to get branded with the scolding iron insignia that lies upon the chest of their leader. Ebonyr watched for hours, planning, scheming. She was trying to calculate the best way to save the prisoners until she realised the extent of the line of the Skane recruits. She knew she could not do this alone. As this thought entered her head she remembered the others. She wanted to be back with them. She remembered the good times she had with them. Her thoughts were interrupted by the screeching of a skane. She whipped her head round to see the deathly stare of a single skane, one by one all the Skanes in centre turned to see her crouching in the trees. They all ran towards the trunk some climbed while some hacked at the trunks with their claws of iron. Ebonyr turned and ran she knew she could not outrun them but she thought that maybe she could outsmart them. As she ran, she threw daggers behind her with near perfect precision. A dozen Skane bodies fell through the trees angering the horde below. Ahead she saw a river she took her chances and darted for it, although she was under attack the dive from the tree to the water was as graceful as an eagle. She plunged to the bottom of the freezing river turning to see if the Skanes would follow. She was lucky, they did not. She lay there at the bottom watching waiting the water welcomed her, it became a part of her suddenly she realised she no longer needed the air to sustain her. She laid there enjoying the serenity watching the clouds go by.

Ebonyr saw the sun through the break in the trees, it was past midday she did not want to waste daylight any longer. She crawled on to the shore, re-adapting to the air that now filled her lungs. She heard voices far away emanating from the forest. She thought that maybe this could be Orik and the others. Ebonyr walked in the direction of the voices but every time she drew closer it sounded like they were far away again, Ebonyr picked up her pace she ran faster and faster with every step. The night appeared quicker than she thought it would. She knew that they would not want to travel at night. Ebonyr kept running she looked for the flicker of campfire light. She climbed trees she looked everywhere; just as she thought all hope of finding them was lost. She saw it, a campfire in the distance flickering in the wind.

Chapter IX
A Needle In A Haystack

Orik ran after Ebonyr but she disappeared as she became part of the forest.
"You will never catch her," said Ethesir. "She is a Liniech she moves as fast as the wind."
"We must go after her," said Esian.
"Why?" Said Firlorn. "She is a Liniech she can look after herself."
Esian resented him for saying this. He wanted to storm after her. He did not know why he just felt compelled to.
"Come on!" shouted Firlorn. "We must find somewhere safe before nightfall."
"I hate to say it but, he is right," Orik said to Esian.
Reluctantly he joined the group. They walked for hours trying to find the most defensible place. They came to what they assumed must be the most northerly place in the forest as they could see the bottom of the eagles peak mountain. They decided to set up camp here for a while as they had the mountain to their back it would be safest, or so they thought …
Night fell, the group began to rest. Fleck stayed awake to look after the group. He watched as the cutthroat roots unearthed themselves to bask in the moonlight their small leaves shone in the moonlight. Fleck gazed in amazement. He thought them beautiful they were bigger than he ever imagined. He had heard stories of their viciousness but he never thought that they would be this beautiful. They danced around enjoying the night, they didn't look vicious at all. They were enticing, mesmerizing almost. Fleck rose from his seat and slowly walked towards them, as he drew closer he realised just how tall they were. They stretched taller than him and had no eyes

that Fleck could see anyway. He got even closer, the heads of the roots snapped round facing him directly, their graceful movement suddenly stopped. Fleck froze unable to move as if fear itself had wrapped him in a rope.

**

Day broke over the mountains like the sea on the cliffs. Orik awoke to see the group of men standing in a circle not far from where they slept. He walked up to them eager to find out what they were doing as he entered into the circle he saw the reassembled body of Fleck the shock of this pushed him back, he nearly lost his footing. The ground was wet with his blood. Flecks limbs had been separated from his body. The slices were faultless perfectly straight through the joints that attached his legs and his arms. The faces of the men were wet with tears.
"It must have been a cutthroat root attack, his limbs were everywhere," said Firlorn.
"Why didn't they attack us," said Orik.
Everyone had a puzzled look on their face they could not work it out.
"Because they didn't see us as a threat Cutthroat only attack if it feels threatened," said Ethesir.

The group mourned the death of Fleck it was sudden and unexpected. They buried him at the foot of the mountain. The anger stirred inside of Firlorn he felt responsible for the death of his friend.

Two days passed the group had not yet gathered the motivation to move from their current camp. They stayed and sometimes they sparred against each other just to kill the time. At last Esian stood while everyone was eating.
"What are we doing? Why are we sitting here doing nothing?

Ebonyr is missing Fleck is DEAD! We should be out there hunting the enemy and finding Ebonyr."

"Aye, I'm with you laddy," Orik said. One by one the rest of the company joined. They started packing up their camp and began to move.

"Let's go back to new town," Firlorn said.

"Good idea maybe Ebonyr went there," said Esian.

"No she would not have been that stupid, a Lienich walking through the open streets of New Town," said Ethesir. "But I do like the idea of going back to restock our supplies."

"But which way is it?" asked Lomak.

The company walked off into the forest trying to keep their sense of direction. They walked for a day without incidence.

"There must be another days walk maximum before we reach the border." Said Orik.

"I would wager," said Esian.

The group decided to make camp where they stood. Esian laid a deer on the floor that he had hunted.

"I'll take care of this," said Orik rubbing his hands in anticipation. That night the company feasted like they were in a grand hall. A rustle came from the bushes. The men shot up and each knocked an arrow in their bows. White light shone from the bushes.

"WAIT!" shouted Orik the others were shocked when they saw what came through the bushes. It was Ebonyr she waded through the shrubbery and sat next to the group as if nothing had happened, she took a bite of the food in front of her, the others couldn't believe their eyes joy filled Esian's heart but their joy was interrupted...

"There is a camp, legions of Skanes reside there."

said Ebonyr "And the dwarf he is there too."

The fear took over the faces of the group. They could not fathom how they have amassed in such a short period of time.

The group walked into new town and headed for 'The Poison Oak Inn.' As they crossed the threshold into the main bar...

"Orik my friend!" shouted Vigor from behind the bar. "A pint of cutthroat for all your company, on the house."

"No thank you." Orik said, "No cutthroat for us tonight, could we please just have the new town homebrew." The confused barman rushed about getting the ten pints ready at once. The group sat down and discussed what they must do hours went by. They had lost themselves in their own conversation. They were alone now not even Vigor was present. Plans were made and cast aside as quickly as they came.

Not one of them could think of a good way to unite the people of Arien and lead them again the new army of Skanes.

"The dwarf," exclaimed Darek. The others looked at him in confusion. "We kill the dwarf, he is their leader right so we get rid of him and then boom the Skanes will fall into chaos." The rest nodded their head the only obstacle was how to get close enough to kill him. Any time they had seen him he had an entourage of at least forty Skanes.

The light shone through the cracked fragment in the glass. It burst through the room highlighting the dust that lay in the air. The group awoke and went downstairs for breakfast. After a quick chat, they decided to each split up and go to the land they called home to try and get other warriors or even an army to try and take down the danger that they all faced. They knew time was not on their side so they agreed to meet up here three months hence.

Esian went back to his homeland, Noragor. While Orik, Darek, and Ebonyr went to Aramoth. Firlorn's men went with Ethesir to Reik to try and gather more weapons. They all said their goodbyes then went their separate ways.

Chapter X
A shroud lifted

It was a normal day in Aramoth the birds sang. the sun shone. The dwarfs went by their daily business tending to their lands. Drunken shouts could be heard from the tavern, The heart in. Intoxicated dwarves wrestled outside to show their prowess. Three dwarves sat around a small table inside the inn. Kindr, Ogork, and Freega.
"Have any of you seen Orik of late?" Asked Freega the others told him that they hadn't.
"Do you suppose that maybe he has just left," said Kindr.
"So that forge is now unmanned you say?" Said Ogork.
"Please, Ogork you're a fighter now a blacksmith as well? You wouldn't even know where to start" said Kindr.
"Who said anything about being a blacksmith," Ogork replied. The three hatched a plan to enter Orik's house and loot it the night after next.

The moon rose, there was a cold bite in the air. Rain fell on Aramoth wetting the faces of the amateur buglers, their breath hung in the air, their hands shook. Sweat mixed with the rain on their faces as they walked towards Orik's house. As Kindr lifted his hand to smash the back window they heard drums coming from the east. The ground started to shake the sound of what sounded like a hundred footsteps rode on the wind into the village.
" Up there!" Shouted Ogork. The trio looked up towards the hill. They saw rank upon rank of Skanes. They numbered 70 strong at least. The ranks jumped down from the hill one by one. The sky was polluted with the firelight that erupted from

the village. Ogork, Kindr, and Freega grabbed what weapons they could and stormed toward the beasts as fast as they could, knowing full well they could not attack a force that size and live. They plunged headlong into the Skanes axes flew, blows were exchanged and alas the battle was over in mere minutes.

The quaint village folk of Aramoth were no match for the attacking force. They were overwhelmed before dawn. In the nights that followed the Skanes and their leader set up Aramoth as their new base camp. They hacked down the surrounding trees and fashioned them into walls around the borders of Aramoth. The walls were ugly, sharp and meant to discourage anyone who looked at them. The Skanes used the blood of the slain dwarfs to paint their insignia on the gate. They bloodied the tips of the spikes they had laid out protruding from the walls to affirm their wickedness. The dwarf leader chose this place for a reason it was out of the way enough that it would have very few visitors and if any tradesmen or anyone of the like was to come near. He could simply kill them. He also chose this place as it was close enough to the rest of the world that he could plan his attack on the Liniech's home with great efficiency.

Days went by and the Aramoth was made uglier and uglier. Houses were turned into the abomination that is a skane dwelling, jagged edges and pikes with severed heads of the previous residents protruded from the sides. The floor was laden with blood, the Skanes played in the puddles of blood like children in rain puddles. A circle had formed in the centre of Aramoth as the hunters had returned with the meals for that night. There was a single Skane that had no bounty. The dwarf leader walked up to this Skane looked him dead in the eye and took his head off with one fell swing of his sword. A roar erupted from the onlooking crowd.

"I will have no weakness here! Only our enemy is weak" shouted the leader.

As Orik walked towards the crest of the hill excitement grew inside him as he longed to look again at his beautiful home village. A stench lied heavy in the air, a foul stench of burnt flesh. Orik's face dropped as he ran to the top of the hill tears flying from his face, he dropped to his knees as he gazed upon Aramoth, the new stronghold of the Skanes. Darek ran beside him, took his sword and sprinted towards the enemy. Ebonyr glided in front of him as if the wind itself carried her.
"No, not now," she said. Orik was paralysed by grief the melting faces of the burning dwarfs poisoned his mind, anger stirred inside him, his dead eyes stared at the dying village for hours. A new emotion within him was the prevalent feeling at the time. Hate. It is something he had not felt before. It was not a comfortable feeling but at this moment in time, Orik revealed in It. He was livid with it and this made him dangerous. Darek and Ebonyr tried to comfort Orik. They put their hands on his shoulders. In his rage, he pulls his axe and points it at them furiously.
"Don't, just don't," he said.
"What are we going to do?" Asked Ebonyr.
"What about Rundon?" Asked Darek "They must be warned."

Midnight struck, the two dwarves and the Liniech still sat upon the hill. In the dead of the night, they could hear the deafening sound of the Skanes feasting. Orik kept his eye on the village, out of the main house he saw their dwarf leader walking out to relieve himself in the bushes. Now that Orik had the time to study him he noticed something familiar about him. As Orik came to his realisation of who this leader was he turned around and revealed that it was an enemy Orik thought harmless an enemy he thought did not have the intelligence. As the dwarf leader turned he revealed that it was Bolger an old acquaintance of Orik's. Orik stood up in anger preparing the release his frustration on Bolger.

Bolger looked up at the hill and raised the alarm. He dispatched a group of ten Skanes to fetch the intruders. Orik and his friends made their escape with haste. They ran for Rundon hoping that somehow they would make it but they knew in their heart that they could not outrun the Skanes. They knew that at some point they would have to fight. They found themselves outside the windmill on the hill where old man Rangor used to live. They braced themselves for battle hoping that somehow they would be able to fight off the onslaught. The Skanes stop short of the trio. The two groups stare at each other savouring the hate that drives them. The two groups ran at each other at breakneck speed. Suddenly a man burst out of the door of the windmill.
"Quickly In here!" He shouted. Orik and his friends ran into the windmill. They shut the door and waited for the Skanes to follow. The windmill was made out of old dark wood, it stretched up high with circular windows on either side. It twisted and turned as it became part of the forest. There were three floors on the top floor there was a small balcony leading from a bedroom, a small chair and table sat upon it. Outside the front door a small garden if you could call it that, burnt out trees and scorched ground lay there, there were tales the spread throughout Arien the children had once gone there to play and but were never seen or heard from again.
Ebonyr went up to a window on the second floor and watched as the Skanes slowly walked up to the entrance to the garden. Something must have spooked them they turned around and bolted back in the direction of Aramoth.
"Thank you," said Orik. "Who are you?"
"I am Rangor," he replied. His face was pale with no marks or blemishes. He was young looking but he had a physique of an old man. He wielded a walking stick that was etched with

many ancient runes.

"No, you're not. I used to hear stories of Rangor when I was a boy. I heard the ancient tales of him going toe to toe with the mayor of New Town to send the armies into the forest of Nosver to vanquish the beasts that call it home. But when the mayor said no he went alone and fought the evil in there but when he returned the mayor sent him into exile. So you see you cannot be him it would make you 400 years old at least."

"Trust me boy it's me." Rangor said "Where else would I have got these." he lifted the back of his t-shirt to reveal layers and layers of scars. Skane bites and slashes received from the vicious cutthroat root.

"But how can this be you don't look at day past 30?" Asked Darek. As the Skanes are massing again Rangor decides to reveal the truth of who he is.

"Well, young dwarf you see I am part of an immortal race that have called this land home for many years but now we number just two. When the dwarfs first settled into Arien. We were hunted and killed. The dwarfs feared us and what we could do. It always puzzled me, I always liked being alone never wanted to interfere with anyone but it matters not I suppose it is just the greed of the dwarfs." Orik took offence to this. He gestured to the others that they should leave. Rangor asked them to stay a while and replenish their food and rest their heads.

Ebonyr listened to the sound of the dwarfs snoring, it kept her awake so she decided she would get some fresh air. As she wandered into the frightfull garden of the windmill her thoughts turned to Esian she hoped that he had not gone through the same heartbreak that Orik endured. She found herself missing his company, she missed his passion for their cause. Ebonyr gazed over at a small wood at the foot of the hill and clear as day she could see the golden marble eyes of a single Skane watching her, she knew it would be a scout waiting for them to leave as they were afraid of the windmill. An uneasy feeling came over her, she went back inside and put her head down to sleep.

In the morning Ebonyr woke the dwarves to alert them to the fact that they were being watched all night.
"I know," said Orik. "You didn't think they were just going to let us leave did you?" Ebonyr did not like the fact that she had been outsmarted by a dwarf but she let it go. She had grown quite fond of this particular dwarf. A knock at the door alerted the immortal who was reading on the upstairs balcony. Rangor walked downstairs and cautiously opened the door, a small conversation took place and then he let in whom he thought was a friend. Orik drew his sword as Bolger walked through the threshold.
"He is unarmed," said Ebonyr.
"I have come to talk," said Bolger. "I have come to give you, and your kin a chance to join me. You will relish in the spoils of our raids and want for nothing." Fear and temptation entered their minds they had seen the death and destruction he was capable of.
"No," Orik said. "I would rather die fighting on the side of good than live well on the side of evil." The others nodded in agreement.
"Now get out before I separate your vile head from your despicable body," said Ebonyr.
Bolger turned and walked away whistling as he did so.

The conversation over a hasty breakfast was originally light-hearted but soon turned to more pressing matters.
"We should leave for Rundon as soon as we can," said Orik.
"Will you come with us Rangor?" Asked Darek. Rangor shook his head he did not want to get himself involved. He was quite all right living in solitude on the hill. Breakfast was finished so the trio decided it was time they got going. They said their

goodbyes to the ancient immortal and left. They walked down the hill and across the river and into the borders of Rundon. Farmers were tending their fields and merchants where traipsing their carts into town. Rundon was a large but strange village it was not the home of one race but men and dwarves also called it home. They had found a way to co-exist, this was thanks to the earl of Rundon, Abathorth. He sat in a great hall in the centre of town, It was made of fine wooden planks detailed with gold. Dragon heads detail the apex of the archway into the hall. Inside great statues stand guard over the walkway to the Earls chair. This char was not as grand as those that one would normally find in great halls of kings but a simple chair detailed with fine furs and fabrics. Abathorth had managed to make the dwarves and the men see that fighting against each other was pointless It was far more lucrative to pull their resources together and strive towards a better life.

Orik and his friends walked to The Broken Axe Pub. They found a small table in the corner and started to talk about how to go about getting an audience with Earl Abathorth. Darek went up the barman and asked him.
"No one gets granted an audience without going on the waiting list. He hears his people every day for an hour at midday." said the barman. A plan was hatched to crash tomorrows counsel session.

A new day dawned and the trio woke up early in the morning and prepared for what might be a very big mistake. They had heard that the Earl was a reasonable man but they still did not want to anger him. Ebonyr thought about how nice it was to go and just buy their food rather hunting in the wild for food. Darek went for a walk around he was trying to soak in the previous couple of weeks and how much he wanted to go back to the way things were. He was not a fighter he did not feel like he could offer anything to anyone. His thoughts turned to Bolger and the offer he had made. He thought that maybe if he joined with him he would be able to barter for the safety of his friends. He did not like the thought of siding with the enemy, but he did not like the thought of being run down and killed even more. Darek decided it would be best to wait for the outcome of the meeting with Earl Abathorth before he made his decision. Orik sat in The Broken Axe thinking about what he was going to say the Earl when he interrupts him giving advice to his people. He knew that for some reason the other two looked at him as their leader. He did not know why but he knew their real leader was back in Noragor. He thought of Esian often he thought about how he could really do with his counsel.

Midday broke over the rustic village. The dwarf and the Liniech met with Orik at the pub. They decided to walk to the hall, on their way they noticed that the streets got busier and busier. In the courtyard in front of the Earl's hall, a large crowd gathered, all shouting, trying to have their say. The guards that stood either side of the Earl shouted for silence.
"Who is first on the list there who requires my counsel, or help," said Earl Abathorth, his voice was loud and booming. An old woman stepped forward.
"I do lord, my son and I do not have enough food for the winter, all I ask is a permit so my son can hunt the land?"
"I cannot give you permission to do that we must let the land flourish by its self," said Earl Abathorth. "but I can do better" as he said this a guard came out of the hall bearing a hamper of vegetables and meats. The elderly woman fell to her knees and burst into tears, the generousness of the Earl of the struck the hearts of Orik and his friends. Orik swallowed his fear and as the next person was called he stepped forward.
"Yes Lord, I need your help and the help of your soldiers, my name is Orik of Aramoth I beseech you, please, lead an attack force towards Aramoth it has been taken over by a

small force of Skanes. They killed the residents and took the village as their home. They are led by the mercenary Bolger I believe that he is from here. Do you know him?"
"I hear you Orik of Aramoth and I am aware of the scourge that defaced your village but my scouts tell me that we do not yet have a sizeable force to attack Aramoth and succeed. As recompense, I would like to invite you and your friends to feast in my hall tonight." Orik did not like that he would not help but he held his plea until the feast.

Orik and his friends went into the market that day. The attire in which they were currently dress were not at all suitable for the great hall of the earl. They bought the best fabrics that they could afford. Ebonyr was dressed in a beautiful white linen dress, with golden accents around the neck and sleeves. Orik and Darek wore matching tunics of a regal blue. When they walked into the great hall, the smell of the feast hit their nostrils, Abathorth invited them to sit.

"So Orik I can't imagine that you were happy with what I decided to do hmm?" he said.
"No, I have to say I was not. I don't understand surely there is something you can do to avenge the people of Aramoth. I think its disgusting how you can turn your back so easily on your neighbours. Aramoth and Rundon have been trading partners for generations....." Orik's rant went on until he no longer had any breath to spare.
"Are you finished master dwarf?" Abathorth said Orik nodded in frustration. "I am setting up a recruitment drive for the Rundon army and I would like you three train them, what say you?"
"We can't train anyone we can barely fight ourselves," said Orik.
"You are the dwarf that journeyed into Nosver alone and survived?" asked Abathorth.

"That's all I need to know for you to train my troops."

Chapter XI
Three months in the making.

Time drifted by and the number of trainees for the Rundon army grew. In return for the training given Orik and his friends received a roof over their heads and food in their bellies. The Earl also gave them a little bit of spending money as well. The groups that they had to train got larger and larger as the months passed. Soon they had a fighting force of at least 200 men and dwarfs trained to a basic level. Darek and Orik along with the dwarf captains appointed by Abathorth train the dwarf regiment while Ebonyr trained the men. They had segregated the two races because while there would be no problem with them fighting side by side each race had different fighting styles and assets. The dwarf soldiers were outfitted with stout heavy iron armour, a kite-shaped shield and sword, they also had at their disposal a selection of throwing axes attached to their hip and back. The men were dressed in slightly lighter armour in colours of green and brown they were outfitted with fighting knives but their primary weapon was to be the bow and arrow. Small throwing knives were held in sheaths attached to their wrists.

Two months had passed and soon it was time for Orik, Darek, and Ebonyr to return to new town to meet their comrades. In the two months that had passed Rundon had expanded into a small town of its own, large walls ran around the perimeter, watch tower kept a watchful eye on the borders of Rundon. Dwarf guards patrolled around while archers stayed up high in the towers. It was the eve of the day that Orik and his friends would have to make the journey back to new town. In the time that they had been training the Rundon Fighting Force, they had themselves become better warriors. Orik was now very competent with his axe, Darek was able to give Orik back his sword as Abathorth had gifted him a full arsenal of weapons, swords, axes, daggers, and a shield. Earl Abathorth put on a feast on their last night.

At this feast, he presented each of them with a new backpack for their journey.

"Now you are sure that you do not want an escort?" said Abathorth. "Maybe you could bring back your friends and we could mount this assault upon the scum that infests Aramoth. Also before you go I would like to officially offer you rank in our fighting force. I offer all of you the rank of captain." Orik and the other each thanked the Earl graciously. The meal was finished and the trio retired to their rooms and tried to get a good night's sleep for they had a long journey the following day.

The sun rose on a new day over Rundon, the fishermen left their boats, merchants left their stores. They all came to the centre of Rundon to bid goodbye to their new captains. Orik, Darek, and Ebonyr were all dressed in their new captain's armour for the occasion. They walked through the crowd shaking the hands of the civilians and soldiers alike. Finally, they came to the Earl standing before them just before they turned on the path that would take them to New Town. He stood in front of them and said,

"We march on Aramoth at dawn on the last day of the month. I hope that you will return by then." he shook their hands and sent them on their way.

As they walked Darek's thoughts returned to Bolger's offer he was scared and he didn't want to betray his friends but his fear was consuming him he thought he would feel better after his experience in Rundon but again he was wondering what his life would be like in league with Bolger.

"Look." said Ebonyr she was gesturing towards a deer that

crossed their paths, slowly she drew a knife from her new wrist brace, in one fluid motion threw it and pierced it through the eye. The deer dropped to the ground with a thud. Ebonyr looked at Orik.

"All yours," she said. Orik walked up to the deer and slung it over his shoulder. As night fell Darek started a fire as Ebonyr readied the camp for sleeping and Orik started to prepare the deer. As they feasted they heard the screech of Warbles nearby. All of them were alert. They all had weapons in hand. Watching. Waiting. The rustling in the bushes put them all on edge. Orik wandered towards the bushes, using his axe to search the bushes for foes. Darek heard the beginning of a warble screech behind him he grabbed his throwing axe and slung it in the same direction. The sound of the axe hitting the floor filled him with dread. Soon after a 10-foot Warble leaped out of the bush throwing Darek to the floor. Orik threw his battle axe hitting the Warble in the shoulder giving Ebonyr time to get close to the beast, she grabbed the back of its head slicing its throat, pouring the thick purple blood onto Darek's head. The rest of the night went without a hitch.

It took them three more days to get to New Town. They walked along the cobbled stone streets and entered The Poison Oak Inn and sat at the table that they sat in when they left. Vigor walked up to them and asked what drink they would like the two dwarves replied with the New Town homebrew and Ebonyr just wanted water. They sat there and drank maybe a little too much. Time passed and there was no sign of Esian or the group of men. They decided to go to bed and maybe they would turn up tomorrow.

Esian walked through the threshold of The Poison Oak Inn in the early hours of the morning. Vigor supplied him with breakfast and a nice cold water. Esian was battle scarred and bloody, Vigor fetched wet towels and a bowl of warm water.

Slowly Esian cleaned his wounds wincing as he did so. The bloody water soaked into his shirt, sticking to his wounds, as he took off his shirt it ripped the wounds that had scabbed and began to bleed. The cries of Esian woke Orik in a fright, he bolted downstairs worried that there was trouble and then he saw the blood ridden body of Esian sitting in the corner, the bar was empty, Vigor and Orik both helped to patch up their injured friend.

"I don't think I have ever seen you without a scratch, my friend," said Orik as he chuckled.

"I think it's the way I look," said Esian. Orik enquired what had happened to him. When Esian returned to Noragor he was met with much hostility, the locals of his home city had heard about his venture and because he helped a dwarf they took offence. They thought it was dishonourable for a man to be in league with a dwarf. They chased him out of town and cornered him against a mountain nearby. They tied him up and tortured him, they branded the mark of shame upon his back. For a whole month, he stayed captured staving being fed scraps every day. The was lucky to receive food for some days he would go without. One day a small child caught his eye as he was having his public weekly lashing in the city square. This child could not watch, the small boy could not contemplate the cruelty that was being dealt upon his own kind, he shut his eyes as the very sight made his stomach turn. One night while Esian was slumped in the corner of his cell the child visited. He came bearing the keys to his cell and set him free. Esian was worried about what they would do to the boy if they found out they had freed him. He asked the boy to come with him but the boy just smiled, turned and left. Esian confused and barely conscious walked for the dock with all the strength he could muster.

"And then I walked here" continued Esian. In the time it took to tell his story Darek and Ebonyr had come down and listened while they ate their breakfast.

"That sounds awful." said Orik. "We have managed to gather a small army in Rundon. Aramoth is the new centre of the Skane army. Their leader's name is Bolger he is a dwarf mercenary that used to supply the surrounding town and villages with the cutthroat root to make their ale It appears that this was not enough for him. I have known Bolger a long time, he has always been arrogant but I thought he was harmless."

"Where are Firlorn and his men?" asked Esian.

"They have not come," said Ebonyr as Vigor brought more drinks and snacks they wondered whether they had abandoned their cause.

"So I suppose we better make way to Rundon then," said Esian.

"Not today my friend you have been through enough today you should rest," said Orik.

The night air of New Town was still brigands were still drinking in the inn a small attack force of Skanes moved unseen through the narrow streets they moved as if they were one with the shadows. They sat outside The Poison Oak Inn watching, waiting for the drunkards to leave. The moon had passed its highest point by the time they all left. Slowly the Skanes moved in they crept passed the door hiding beneath tables and behind supports as Vigor moved around the bar cleaning the tables and collecting the glasses. Vigor, after finishing all his work, retired to his bed.

Upstairs Esian had awoken, hearing footsteps coming up the stairs unable to get out of bed he grabbed his dagger and waited. He watched the door fearful of what might be the other side. The footsteps stopped at his door. As the door creaked open Esian received the dead stare of the Skane that stood there. Esian threw his dagger but his vision was blurred for he was disabled with pain. He could hear the commotion of other skirmishes from around the inn. The Skane leaped for him and pinned him to the bed as it lifted its claw to slash Esian's throat

away. Vigor had crept up behind it with a swift thrust he buried Esian's dagger in its back. As the Skane fell to the floor Orik, Darek and Ebonyr ran into the room ready to fight.
"Will somebody please tell what is going on here?" said Vigor. Darek then explained what was happening in the world over a nice cup of tea.

A week passed and it was time for Orik and his friends to start making their way as it was nearing month end. As Vigor watched them leave New Town he wished he could go with them, he wanted to help. They decided to walk through the night as time was against them and they had to get to Rundon. The cold night wind blistered against their faces. They made good time, they crossed the borders of Rundon before dawn. The large north gate of Rundon was closed a dwarf guard approached them. As he started to inquire who they were a spark of recognition flew across his face.
"Captains my apologies I did not recognize you. Who is your friend?"
"His name is Esian he is with us and he will fight with us," said Orik. The guardsman opened the gate.

Rundon had changed in the week that they had been away. There were more soldiers in the streets and it was clear that they were mustering for battle. Orik, Darek, and Ebonyr went to see each of the squads that they were in charge of, just to check in on them and make sure that they were all still up to scratch. That afternoon they ran through a couple of combat drills before they went to see Earl Abathorth. The Earl welcomed them with a huge feast.
"In two days time, we will attack Aramoth, to try and prevent the Skane scum from spreading. We have kept a watch on the village and they have been sending out raiding parties almost every night and they have been returning with prisoners. My scouts have told me that they have been setting the prisoners

free in the woods close by and hunting them for sport." said Earl Abathorth. The disgust was obvious on the faces of his guests. He told them the plan he had formulated to try and overwhelm the enemy.

"I have thought that we will put the dwarf regiment up front to face the enemy head on a try and lure them out and when they have fully engaged our dwarves we will sound a retreat and then the men will creep up the hill and rain down on them with arrows.

Chapter XII
Best Laid Plans

The day of the assault arrived. The army of Rundon marched upon the fallen village of Aramoth. They arrived at the break of day, Orik and Darek stood in front of their respective squads as did the other captains. Earl Abathorth walked up and down reassuring the men and inspecting them as he did so. He took his place in front of his army and watched as rank upon rank Skanes formed but Bolger was no were to be seen. Soon enough the ranks broke and through came Bolger. He walked up to Abathorth and said.
"Do you think this is wise my lord you are outnumbered two to one and we all know that no one matches a Skane for furiousness." He started to shout "What hope have the men of Rundon got against the Skane brethren. How can you possibly hope to overcome such a force...." his words were cut short.
"We will destroy you, for we have something that you don't, loyalty do you really think that when it is all said and done your Skanes will still be loyal to you?" said Orik as he stood face to face with Bolger. "I think not." Bolger turned and walked away, he disappeared into the sea of the hateful lizard men.

The sky darkened, rain clouds formed overhead. Soon the cold droplets fell on the heads of the dwarfs. The crack of thunder made those in the army, of a particularly nervous disposition jump. The Skanes started the screech and scream they tried to intimidate the wall of armour that stood before them. The training that Orik and Darek had given them set in and soon the dwarfs had created an impenetrable shield wall. A horn was blown from deep inside Aramoth. It was a charge horn soon all of the Skanes sprinted towards the dwarfs. All of the captains fell into the ranks and lowered their shields to become part of the shield wall. The second rank lowered their spears as the Skane ranks approached. The dwarfs stood their ground as wave upon wave of Skanes stormed their ranks soon after the initial charge. Small gaps were formed behind the line. Where the dwarfs would surround the beasts and pick them off efficiently.

As they were locked in combat Ebonyr and Esian rose to the top of the hill with a legion of tall archers waiting to release their arrows and rid Arien of the filth that lay below. As they got the crest of the hill they saw that nearly half the dwarf force had been depleted. They blew their attack horn for the dwarf force to quickly withdraw, the dwarfs quickly retreated slightly. The men released their arrows and they all flew through the air hitting their mark it completely decimated about ten percent of the Skane force. Esian climbed down the hill and crept into the main house to find Bolger, but he was not there. He looked all around upstairs and down stair looking for the evil fiend but he was no were to be seen. He left the house and searched amongst the battlefield dispatching foes as he made his way to the epicentre. He saw Orik and Darek fighting back to back. He was surprised at the skill and smoothness in which they both handled themselves. He ran to Orik to notify him of Bolger's disappearance. Orik immediately ran to Abathorth and asked him for a small group of dwarfs. To try and find him and hopefully kill him. By this time a group of Skanes had made their way up the hill to confront the archers, in a synchronised movement the front two ranks of the men drew their fighting knives and ran for the Skanes that were darting before them.

Orik and Darek took a group of four dwarf soldiers. Searched the whole village and still could not find him. They realised that he has probably fled the battlefield, they all went up to the hill fighting the remainder of the Skanes. They all spread out searching for him. Ebonyr shouted to the group she could see him and a small group of Skanes darting for Rundon. Ebonyr sprinted after him, she used the wind to carry her there, Orik and Esian ran after her as the soldiers they took with them were locked in combat.

Ebonyr entered the borders of Rundon. The small set of guards that were left behind were dead on the ground. Cautiously she looked around waiting for an attack to come from any direction. She could hear the screams of housewives from across town. As she began to run towards them two Skanes jumped from the rooftop slashing her back as they did so Orik still a league away threw one of his small axes with all his might. It flew past the Skanes, but it distracted them for long enough for Ebonyr, with her last seconds of consciousness slit their throats. Orik and Darek got to Ebonyr in time to watch her fade away her eyes closed as she fainted. "Stay with her," said Orik. The orange glow of the fire was soon projected into the sky. Orik ran towards it saving as many people as he could.

Darek stayed with Ebonyr until help arrived. He sat there on the floor waiting. Her breath became shallow. The beautiful white glow of her skin started to fade. Then out of no were a Skane attacked. Darek was knocked to the floor as he tried desperately to defend his friend but as the Skane had a chance to strike its killing blow. It scooped him up underneath its arm and ran out of town. Abathorth on his way back to Rundon ordered the men he brought with him to fire at the Skane that had Darek under his arm but alas they were too far away and all the arrows fell short. Before he left Abathorth left Orders to his captains that when they had defeated the enemy that half of them were to remain and wipe out any stragglers in the village and the other half was to return to Rundon.

Orik made his way through the burning houses and shops. He tried to find Bolger, soon enough he caught a glimpse of him running for new town. Orik wanted to chase him down but the people of Rundon were more important. He set about finding buckets to fill with water but in his heart, he knew he could not put out this inferno by himself. Orik decided to just get as many people out as he could. He could not believe his eyes at the amount of devastation that this one dwarf has inflicted. He could not help but empathise with the grief of the people that were pouring out of the burning buildings eventually Abathorth reached Orik he told his men to help get the people out, soon after the rest of the army joined them. Abathorth couldn't help but feel a small amount of joy as he knew the return of his army meant that they had been victorious. All of the men and dwarfs ran about the town fetching people and taking them to the river were Esian was looking after the wounded.

The Dwarfs that were left in Aramoth hunted the remainder of the Skanes that had lost their nerve and hid in the disgusting houses they had fashioned. Soon enough they had eradicated the stragglers and then they started to rip down the walls and shacks, Aramoth was not going to be the same anytime soon but at least the soldiers could make a start. Earl Abathorth joined Esian in caring for the wounded. Esian sat with Ebonyr hoping that she would wake up, her skin was dark and her clear blood seeped through every bandage that was put on her. He stayed by her bedside for the days that followed.

Rundon was still smouldering away but most of the buildings had been reduced to ash. The people were now homeless and had nowhere to go. They looked to their leader they wanted to know what he wanted them to do. The people had found a new type of loyalty to their Earl. Soon rumours were started that maybe they will go to New Town for aid but some want to try and rebuild the now deserted Aramoth. Earl Abathorth thought about it since the battle was over, it was a subject that had kept him awake for the past couple of days, but he had finally come to a decision about what to do. He took the advice of Esian who said that they should take up residence in Aramoth as to stay in the open air against the elements would risk infection was too great. It would be easier to care for them if they were inside. The soldiers carried the wounded on makeshift stretchers.

Orik's spirit was broken as entered Aramoth it was painful to see his home desecrated like this. Orik and a couple of men were sent ahead of the people of Rundon to clear the battlefield of the dead. They would pile the corpses of the enemy and burn them and then they would bury their comrades. In the weeks that followed everyone came together to rebuild Aramoth. Orik walked to where they were keeping the wounded to visit Ebonyr who still had not awoken.

A tall hooded figure limped through the crowds helping to rebuild Aramoth. His clothes were poor and caked with mud and twigs. As he walked towards the house that kept the wounded out of the cold. He started to utter ancient words although he spoke softly his words were heard throughout the whole village. The sounds resonated through the houses, Orik and Esian both looked up and ran out looking for the origin of the sounds. To their amazement, they both saw a face they recognised. The hooded man pushed them both aside taking no notice of them he stepped up beside Ebonyr, as he did so her skin began to glow again and as the bandages on her back dried her eyes opened.
"Ethesir?" she whispered.
"Welcome back to the world," he said softly as she fell back into a more comfortable sleep.
Esian ran up to Ethesir and embraced him with force.
"Thank you I had lost all hope," he said Orik stood there with a

fierce look on his face.

"Where were you?" he said. "Where is Firlorn?" The old wizard turned around to show Orik his face, it was scared and covered in blood, Ethesir lifted his cloak to reveal that he had lost a leg and replaced it with a wooden peg. Upon returning to Riek a civil war had started between two neighbouring countries, Danoulgey and Olouss. They were both governed by kings that coveted what the other had a war had been brewing for the past 400 years. Ethesir, Firlorn and his men had been fighting to try and get peace between the two and unite them against the Skanes. Ethesir left Firlorn and his men there in an attempt to act as intermediaries between the two kings. The battles that were fought before Ethesir left were brutal and horrific, he had never seen such ruthless hate. He fled the battlefield hoping to find Orik and Esian, he hoped that he could ask them for their help.

"Why?" said Orik "why should we help them it's a fight in a distant land it does not affect us I have seen enough battle for this year"

"but Danoulgey is Firlorn's home and I don't think either of the kings will stop there after either of them have triumphed they will seek to conquer Arien next I am sure of it." said Ethesir "unless they come to terms"

"I would like to remain here and rebuild my home, I am sorry" Said Orik, Esian nodded along, for he would like to stay with his friends and the men and dwarfs he bled within the days passed.

Chapter XIII
A New Dawn

A long year had passed since the battle of Aramoth and it was very nearly rebuilt. The people had decided to build it back bigger as the population from Rundon was a lot more than that of Aramoth, over the year it grew so large It could even be classed as a town. The inn was renamed The Axe and Sword to signify the new bond that was formed between the men and dwarfs. There was a discussion about who should govern the village. Abathorth said to Orik that he should take up the mantle but Orik wanted to return to a simple life he had managed to become the head chef at the Axe and Sword. So Abathorth continued as Earl but he put in place a council that consisted of Orik, Esian, Ebonyr and one of the captains that had survived the battle. Who was known as Nolan? The five of them agreed to meet every week and make decisions about the town and discuss matters of the people.

Esian built himself a house on the hill where he resided with his new wife Ebonyr. They both regretted that they did not manage to get hold of the necklace they both strived for. Rumours had spread that Bolger tried to attack the Liniech stronghold in the barrow mountains and was instantly killed but no one knew of the whereabouts of the necklace. Esian and Ebonyr married six months after the battle for Aramoth with the whole town in attendance, Orik fashioned their rings himself setting a small white gem into the top with their names inscribed on the inside. They lived their life to the fullest hoping one day to start a family if it was possible. Esian was appointed the leader of the force of Aramoth and led with the utter loyalty of his dwarf force and Nolan was his second.

Nolan would reside of the day to day running or the army and Esian would be the one to make the larger decisions.

Earl Abathorth sent out search parties for the missing dwarf Darek every day but he was never found no one had seen him. The Earl sent envoys to New Town in hope of finding someone that had seen him but that also seemed hopeless. He also set up a new trade route between New Town and Aramoth as the earth beneath Aramoth was perfect for farm and growing crops. He also had the bravest warriors in all of Arien so he gave them permission to journey to Nosver and hunt cutthroat root. Ebonyr also paid some of these soldiers to collect leaves from the bloodheart tree as the leaf she used lost its colour and soon went limp and was not suitable for her use. She had already planted a bloodheart tree in the back garden but it had not yet grown.

Orik had rebuilt his house exactly the way it was even with the forge but he let it be used by the team of blacksmiths that came from Rundon. They lived with him also and they enjoyed his company as he did theirs. They would often go hunting together as they all preferred to live off the sweat of their own brow. Orik liked going hunting so he could get all of the best ingredients himself for his kitchen in The Axe and Sword. Most nights Orik sat on the bench outside his house and thought about the small adventure that he had been on. He thought of the friends lost and friends made but most of all he could not get the small dwarf child Fygir. A child who made him realise why he shouldn't be afraid. If that small child with very little knowledge of the world could embrace death with the honour he had then Orik should strive to live with honour the best he could.

**

The battle between Danoulgey and Olouss raged finally King Baracoul of the country Olouss was victorious. He appointed his most trusted Lieutenant, Lork, to run Danoulgey. With Orders to double the size of the army to prepare the assault on Arien Ethesir who was now an adviser to Baracoul pleaded with him to not attack Arien. He threatened to leave if he did so. In anger, Baracoul slashed his sword at Ethesir but before it made contact, he was gone, disappeared into thin air. In his rage, Baracoul doubled the rate at which he was training new soldiers in hope to attack Arien within the year. He was mad with power any time one of his subjects disagreed with him, they were never seen again.

Ethesir appeared in the centre of Aramoth in a flash all of the citizens ran to him curious about the noise. He fell to his knees completely drained of power. As he passed out he uttered a single word.
"Orik" Abathorth ran to Orik's kitchen to notify him of the situation. It took two days for Ethesir to recover and soon he told the council of the danger that soon approached them. The decision was made to try and unite the people of Arien and face this new enemy...

To be continued…

Printed in Great Britain
by Amazon